The ROYALS

Complete Me

GENEVA LEE

The
ROYALS

Complete Me

GENEVA LEE

everafter
ROMANCE

Ever After Romance

www.EverAfterRomance.com

www.GenevaLee.com

First published, 2017. Second edition.

Print ISBN: 9781635765304

Cover Design © Date Book Designs. Image © iktash/Bigstockphoto.com

In loving memory of Suzi,
who will always be a Royal

CHAPTER ONE

WASHINGTON D.C.

THE QUEEN'S BEDROOM, considered well-suited to visiting monarchy by the White House staff, felt as stodgy and antiquated as the name suggested. It had certainly received the title when my grandmother wore the crown, because my own wife was anything save boring. Despite the overtly Victorian femininity of the wall-coverings and lacy bedspread, Clara's presence breathed a vitality into the space. She stirred in her sleep and my breath caught even as I felt a familiar restlessness awakening in me.

Her rich, brown hair fanned over the pillowcase as a serenity passed over her fair features, and her lips began to move silently in her dreams. Propping myself up on my elbow, I studied her and wondered who she was talking to. While it might be pointless to be jealous of the time she spent asleep, I couldn't help it. I couldn't possess her in her dreams. For my irrational side—which too often overrode my common sense—it was unbearable.

Maybe that's why I felt the need to wake her so often for nocturnal activities.

The anatomical center of my irrationality twitched in agreement at the thought, and my hand went to it. I stroked myself absently. How early was too early to wake her for morning sex? It was difficult to determine given how cocked up our sleep schedule had been since arriving in Seattle a little over a week ago. Since then we'd visited three more U.S. cities on our goodwill tour. At least the capitol was our last stop. Between traveling and our daughter's teething-induced crankiness, Clara was perpetually knackered.

Still, she never said no.

"Are you warming up for something?" she murmured. Her lashes fluttered as she eyed me drowsily.

"I didn't want to wake you." I didn't add that I would have woken her anyway. Although I took pride in my self-control, I was glaringly deficient in that avenue where it came to my wife. When I had her alone I needed to be touching her.

Clara's laughter lifted some of the never-ceasing weight from my chest. Perhaps my obsession stemmed from the miraculous balm of her presence. She'd always been able to alleviate the burdens I carried with me, even though the pressures in my life had increased exponentially since she came into it. She bound me as she released me. It was the great paradox of our love that we saved each other by chaining ourselves to lives of duty.

"You would have woken me anyway," she accused, stretching her slender arms over her head as she displayed her uncanny ability to read my thoughts.

The movement caught my attention and I seized my chance. Rolling on top of her, I snatched her hands and held them. "Is that a complaint, poppet?"

Her body responded with a comforting awareness of my dominance. Clara's legs fell open, softening in welcome and her breathing shifted to shallow, eager panting as she purred the only words I needed to hear. "Yes, please."

I accepted her invitation, releasing my grip on her only long enough to pluck free the sash that held the bed curtains to the post. She didn't protest as I gently tied her wrist to the bed. Moving my knee against her bare cunt as a gage, I decided she was more than content by the idea of a morning play session.

"I'm not certain Americans approve of bondage so early in the morning." But she stretched her free arm toward the other post even as she spoke.

I couldn't hold back my arrogance as I smirked down at her. "I don't play by their rules."

I cinched her wrists tighter to prove my point and was rewarded with a warm surge of arousal.

"Should the Queen be tied up in her own bedroom?" She loved to rile me up, knowing that it would pay dividends in how rough I'd get. The saucier she got, the more I needed to dominate her. Like most couples our sex life ran the gamut of slow and sensual to clawing and primal. Unlike most couples, it ran that gamut daily.

"If she's in the King's bed, she should be." Sinking back on my heels, I appreciated the sight of my wife tied up and helpless. Thankfully, the house was large and Elizabeth was with the nanny down the hall, because I felt inspired to make her scream. Clara's breasts spilled from her silky nightgown and I snapped the fragile straps to release them entirely. Moving down her body, I sucked the soft mound, drawing her nipple into my mouth. While I might be impatient to get her beneath me, I never minded taking my time once I had her there. Quiet moans escaped from her and I increased my suction until I was practically biting the soft flesh. Clara arched toward me, her hips beginning to wiggle as she searched for relief. I loved watching my wife come but guiding her toward the edge was arguably even better. Turning this beautiful, intelligent woman into mass of incoherent desire was only fair since she reduced me to that primal state every time she walked into a room.

"Don't you have appointments today?" She pressed her body desperately to mine.

"Not for hours," I said with a mouthful of her creamy breast. I hadn't bothered to tell her how early I'd decided to start my day. I had no doubt that the time would pass too quickly for both of our likings.

"X!" she demanded through gritted teeth.

I withdrew and raised an eyebrow. Questioning my authority in the bedroom would only earn her more time on her back. I suspected she knew that. "You're being impatient."

"And you're being infuriating!" Her hands curled over her restraints as if she was testing them.

"Don't think you're getting out of those so easily," I informed her even as I settled between her thighs. Stroking the head of my cock down her swollen seam, I grinned at the amusement she couldn't quite hide from her answering glare. Hoisting her legs around my hips, I held her there, stretching her long body between the bed posts and my groin, and waited.

"Please." She licked her lips, her eyes going glassy as she asked again. "Please. Please."

I groaned, unable to resist her when she began to beg, and thrust inside her. Her muscles immediately contracted around my shaft as I drove her toward release. She cried out, splitting apart. I'd taken her over the edge, but once again she'd brought me to my knees.

THE OVAL OFFICE looked far more ceremonial than official with the camera crew shooting in front of the President's desk. The room itself was decorated in shades of ivory and yellow, but the color palette did little to warm the cool atmosphere. It wasn't unreasonable for the White House to film my visit, but it didn't lend itself to natural conversation. Having never met the new Commander-in-Chief of the United States, I had to be on my best behavior. I only hoped he would be as well.

GENEVA LEE

"Alexander, welcome." President Williams tipped his head in a small greeting as he rose from his chair. It was acknowledgment of our shared power, but not a bow. For that I was grateful. If there was one thing I loved about America, it was that no one routinely felt the need to prostrate themselves in my presence.

Williams was about the age of my father, but the two had never officially met. He'd taken office shortly before the assassination that claimed the King's life. But age is where the similarities ended. Albert had been quintessentially British in his looks and demeanor. At least, in public. Williams was every bit the American head of state right down to the red power tie. Despite his years, the lines on his face only gave him an air of wisdom that matched his salt and pepper hair, and, like most Americans foisted into the spotlight, he looked more like a movie star than a bedraggled politician. He was the on-camera commander, whose power was limited by the large congress of lawmakers also elected by the people. That was one position we were both in.

"Congratulations on your ascension. I had hoped to share your joy, but after the wedding, it was felt that..." He trailed away, allowing my memory to recall the events of my wedding day.

"Of course." I allowed a tight smile. It was polite to offer his solicitations, naturally, but no matter how much time had passed I had never put my wedding day behind me. Williams had been in attendance for the ceremony. Considering the circumstances, he, along with several other powerful dignitaries, had sent their regrets when invited to my coronation. I couldn't blame them. If I could have skipped the ritual I would have, too. "We've been negligent, as well. Clara and I planned to visit your country much earlier. Life and politics got in the way."

"Don't they always?" He gestured to a chair next to his, and I took it. "What is your lovely wife up to today?"

"Motherhood," I said stiffly. Clara would not always be able to avoid the camera, but for the time being I was content to enable her desire to stay off screen. I still hadn't warmed to the idea of sharing her with the world.

"I feel certain our special relationship would be even more special now that you're married to an American," the president said light-heartedly as he adjusted his suit coat before taking his seat.

Annoyance surged through me, and I did my best to hide it. This man and this country had no claim to my wife. I couldn't exactly tell him that though, especially not during a televised interview. "I think you'll find that Clara is as American as I am."

We laughed, but neither of us were amused. Williams's predecessor had been known for his ease in awkward situations. It hadn't been a strong enough quality to get him reelected. Now the atmosphere in the Oval Office had the same wary tension of an impending cock fight. This was what happened when you put two alpha males into a room. There was no punchline, only a quiet struggle for power.

"I heard she prefers coffee," the Secretary of State joined in, her tone effusive. At least, Williams had appointed someone adept at dismantling tension to his cabinet. It was a particularly keen appointment since she handled most of the administration's foreign policy.

"I'm working on that," I admitted. The good-natured ribbing had the intended effect and the conversation shifted into an easygoing conversation between the heads of two sovereign nations. About an hour later, during a rousing debate between the merits of American football versus European football, the camera crews began to dismantle their equipment.

"This way, please," an aide showed the crews out of the office, and the atmosphere changed again.

Williams slumped in his seat, switching off his on-camera persona and becoming another man. "Scotch?"

"Please."

A moment later, an aide dutifully delivered the drinks as a young, nervous man joined us.

"Alexander, allow me to introduce my press secretary Richard May. He's here to keep us on track for the press conference."

I rose and shook the man's hand as he declined the offering of a Scotch. "I do apologize for sticking you back in front of a camera so soon."

"I was born in front of a camera," I said flatly. It wasn't technically true, but it may as well have been. I'd never known what it was like to be in public without someone filming me. My only real sanctuary from that fact had been during my time on the war front.

"Of course," May said absently as he shuffled through

some papers. "I imagine that most of their questions will be fairly soft. They'll ask about Clara and your daughter."

I forced myself to nod. Despite my desire to keep my wife and child out of the spotlight, it was futile. I did my best to keep a firm line when it came to the press though, especially given how vicious the media had been during our courtship. As much as possible, I wanted Elizabeth to have a normal life, however unlikely the possibility was.

"Then there's the Edward issue."

"I hope you're speaking about an upcoming magazine article." This time I didn't bother to hide my annoyance. I'd been warned by own people that this might be brought up abroad.

"We've briefed the corps on the topics that they're allowed to broach," the president assured me, "but freedom of the press means we can't tell them what they can ask."

I didn't miss the none-too-subtle dig. "Britain has it as well."

"Then you know the trouble it can cause." Williams spread his hands apologetically, and I nodded.

There had been some negative attention regarding my brother's engagement in the tabloids. But Edward's decision to come out of the closet had been largely met with enthusiasm. For most it signaled that the monarchy was no longer an archaic relic, but there were always dissenters.

"I'm prepared to take the fifth," I joked, doing my best to sound as if the subject didn't irk me.

"I think he'll do just fine." Williams winked at May. "Are we ready then?"

May trembled a little as he nodded his head. There wasn't enough anti-anxiety medicine in the world to counter the stress of his job. It was remarkable that the man was allowed in front of the camera. As we headed toward the briefing room, Williams lagged behind. I took the signal and followed suit.

"I am sorry that we weren't at your coronation." It was a surprisingly sincere apology for a man who had fought to command the room when we first met. "Our security teams felt the risk outweighed the duty, and, speaking man to man, my first concern is always for my wife."

"It's understandable." I could appreciate a man putting his wife first. Where my own safety was concerned, I rarely cared, but I'd surround Clara with an army if she'd allow me. "If it were up to me, Clara wouldn't have come either."

Williams tugged at his necktie, and I realized he was holding something back. After a few seconds, he continued. "Our reports suggest that there might have been a larger plot in the works."

"Ours as well." So it wasn't just the British Secret Service concerned over the assassination. Our troubles had caught the attention of the CIA, too.

"I'm happy to pass along the intelligence we have. I'm sorry to say that most of the information hasn't panned out."

"Please," I accepted tersely. Then it wasn't just their trails that had gone cold, but ours as well. It was tempting to believe that the threat to my family had ended with the murder of Jack Hammond. The problem with accepting it was that someone had seen fit to murder the man who by all accounts was responsible for my father's death. If Smith Price, my personal source of information within Hammond's network, hadn't been the one to take Hammond's life—as he claimed—then someone else had been.

"Unless you already have him…" Williams left the thought hanging in the air. It seemed whatever information he had was unlikely to provide new insight.

"That's the thing about monsters," I told him as we stopped outside the briefing gallery. "You cut off one head, only to discover there's another one."

"That I understand."

Both our countries had faced dark times of late. I could imagine the threats to his family were as significant and omni-present as my own. Without thinking, I clapped a hand on his shoulder in a show of solidarity—and perhaps, comfort. Williams's face showed he understood.

"They're ready for you, sir," an aide advised.

I couldn't quite prevent the grimace that flashed over my face, but I replaced it with a smile as I stepped in front of the rows of reporters. May stayed by my side to direct the chaos as they began to call out to me.

"Miss Bernstein," May said and a woman shot up from her chair. She didn't bother adjusting her skirt or flipping her hair, instead her eyes zeroed in on me.

This is going to sting.

"Your Highness, will the crown sanction the marriage of your brother?"

I had been warned, so I kept my face passive. It was no surprise that they were going after Edward. I couldn't expect one of the most ruthless free presses in the world to ask what type of biscuit I preferred. My father would have taken the woman's head off, but I'd already decided to take a different approach. I'd kill them with charm. Ignoring the rage coursing through me, I smiled. "I already have."

This incited a barrage of follow-ups from the crowd, but I held up a hand before May could step in. "I'd like to limit topics to policy and my country."

Not my family. They were off-limits—all of them. I'd lost too many of the people close to me to share the ones I had left. If I had to give every part of me away to protect my family, I would.

There was a moment of squirming silence while the journalists regrouped.

"There's a vocal minority in Parliament who would like to see the monarchy abolished. How will you respond if support for the initiative gains momentum?" an intrepid man called out.

"God save the King," I replied, earning a wave of laughter. The dry response shifted the line of questioning to topics sure to produce amusing sound bites. I did my best to stay clever and steer things away from the people in my life. When I finally took my leave, Williams met me at the door.

"All charm and no concrete answers—you were born for politics."

I supposed it was meant as a compliment. "I was born into politics."

"I guess you never have had much of a choice," he mused as we made our way to the residential rooms. "Your destiny was decided for you."

I thought of Clara and my life before I met her. Every moment of my life propelled me to her, and yet I'd tried to push her away. In the end, we'd decided to fight for one another. That had been a choice—as had my decision to take the throne. It had been a personal decision rather than a forced one. Becoming king allowed me to search for those responsible for the attacks on my wife. In the end, there had always been choices—hard ones. "I've chosen my destiny."

"As have I." Williams paused to say goodbye before returning to his office.

He still had a day of work ahead of him, and I had my whole world ahead of me. I entered the small living suite our hosts had offered us quietly, afraid to wake a sleeping toddler. Instead, a babbling ball of joy toppled toward me as Elizabeth misstepped. In one swift move, I scooped my daughter into my arms.

"I'm sorry, Your Majesty!" Penny, the ever-fussing nursemaid we'd brought along, rushed over to save me, but I held my little girl. The poor woman couldn't fathom that a man would want to care for his child. If it killed me, I would show her that I wasn't simply any man.

Clara looked up from her book and rolled her eyes at the scene developing before her, but she didn't step in.

Later I'd be more than happy to spank her for being mischievous. Her lips curled into a knowing smirk as if she had read my mind again.

"Penny, why don't you take a few minutes for yourself," I advised her.

"Sir?" She stared at me as if this was a test.

"I'd like to be alone with my family," I clarified.

She continued to look distraught, but she curtsied and took her leave.

"Is it so hard to believe that I want to hold my daughter?" I grumbled when we were alone.

"I suppose most kings are interested in furthering their bloodline, not building blocks." Clara's eyes lingered on the two of us as I settled onto the carpet with Elizabeth, who immediately pulled herself up and began practicing her latest trick: walking.

"Clever girl," I praised her. "Already walking."

"She's nearly fifteen months old," Clara pointed out, even as she dropped onto the floor beside me. Soon she was as captivated by Elizabeth's antics as I was. My hand found hers on the carpet. We stayed like that until a familiar form appeared in the doorway. Norris looked as proud as any grandfather as he surveyed my family, but when I lifted my gaze to his, I immediately knew something was wrong.

"I'll just be a few minutes," I murmured to Clara, brushing a kiss over her forehead even as it wrinkled in concern. Norris had given us a fair amount of space during our limited family time. We both knew that his sudden appearance meant news out of England. Getting to my feet, I crossed the room to him, Elizabeth taking dozens of tiny steps to try to catch up with me.

"There's been a development," Norris said under his breath. We both glanced toward Clara who was watching us with wary eyes. She didn't like to be kept out of the loop, a fact which had been a sore point since the day we married. Her contention that we should keep no secrets from each other was valid, but I couldn't bear to burden her with some of the knowledge I carried. She scrambled up and caught Elizabeth as I stepped into the hallway with Norris behind me. I met my wife's eyes for a moment, hoping she understood my need for privacy, before I closed the door.

"Is it about Hammond?" Nearly a year after his murder and we were no closer to the answers that might lead me to our common enemy. Whoever had murdered him hadn't done so as a favor to me. That was becoming clearer with each stone we turned over.

"No. I'm not even certain what it means."

"You're going to have to give me more to go on," I informed him. It wasn't like Norris to be mysterious, which meant that whatever news he had to deliver wasn't good.

"The team combing through your father's personal effects uncovered something."

"That would seem to be good news." When I'd asked for a discreet team to dig further into my father's personal life, I'd hoped to find links to the people responsible for his death. Whatever secrets he'd kept could be the key to discovering the truth about what happened that day.

"I'm afraid it only raises more questions." Norris looked torn and my pulse ratcheted up as adrenaline surged through my blood.

"What did they find?" I forced the question past gritted teeth.

"Not what," Norris corrected gently. "Who."

"Who?" I repeated. "They found a person?"

"They found your brother."

"Edward?" I asked even as sensation of vertigo gripped me.

"No." Norris paused to allow what he was saying to sink in.

"I have another brother?" My words were so strangled I barely recognized my own voice.

Norris drew a deep breath as if steeling both of us for what came out next. "It seems you do, indeed."

CHAPTER TWO

LONDON

*T*he Christmas season was proving to be less a blessing than a headache for Belle's fledgling company. While the business had seen exponential growth in recent months, subscriptions had tripled in the first week of December alone. Thanks, in part, to a number of editorials her partner had managed to arrange in major magazines, but also due to the number of upcoming holiday parties. It seemed that Belle's brain child, Bless—a couture clothing rental company that kept its clients' closets stocked with the latest high end fashion—was headed for success. The trouble was that their operation was quickly outgrowing their office and their two-woman staff.

Lola, her partner and her best friend's little sister, appeared before her with a clipboard. Unlike Belle, who had paired a creamy cashmere jumper from Prada with tight, black trousers and Louboutin flats, Lola was dressed to the nines in a body skimming black Dolce & Gabbana dress that stopped far too short for propriety. The leggy brunette had mitigated this fact by wearing opaque black tights and suede Jimmy Choo boots that came to her knees. She looked as though she might dash from this meeting straight onto the runway. Her make-up was perfect down to the brilliant ruby lipstick she sported. Belle, on the other hand, hadn't bothered with anything but a little mascara and lip gloss. She was too fair and her lashes too blonde to get away without it. She supposed it was a perk of being married that she no longer felt the need to get dolled up every morning, even if she routinely did.

"I leave from New York right after Christmas." Lola began to rattle off her schedule with such speed that Belle redirected her focus so that she caught all the details.

Lola was the face of their fledgling company. She had pushed Belle to be the one to sit for interviews and attend photo shoots, but the founder had decided against it. In a way, Lola was famous in her own right. Whereas her sister was soft and welcoming, Lola was polished with an edge. She was a formidable business woman, and, in the end, it proved to be a marketing coup. Lola Bishop was an it-girl almost overnight. Of course, it didn't hurt that her sister was the Queen of England. What woman wouldn't take fashion advice from her?

It had garnered her a little more attention than they'd planned, however. Lola had found herself the subject of tabloid fodder ever since. If she walked next to a man in public, all the gossip columns speculated if he was the love of her life. Only Belle knew the truth. Lola had sworn off men for the time being, preferring instead to keep her nose to the grindstone and build an empire. There just wasn't time for dating when a girl was out to rule the world. Thankfully, she didn't mind the limelight, which left Belle free to focus on building the business the way she had wanted. It also made her more comfortable.

She'd had no idea when she got involved with Smith Price that her life would change forever. While many good things had come out of it—like the business and their marriage—Belle had also been the target of several attacks aimed to keep her husband under his crooked employer's thumb. They were free of that now, but she was more than happy to stay behind closed doors.

"I also need you to look at those resumes." Lola pointed to the stack of papers she'd printed from an online search. They'd been sitting there for the better part of the week. Apparently, she felt it would take pointing them out before Belle would acknowledge their existence.

"Wow," Belle said, picking up the stack. "It looks like more than a few people are interested in working with us."

"Those are just the contenders," Lola told her proudly.

Belle sifted through them, trying to find the motivation to look.

"We have to hire people," Lola reminded her.

Belle knew that, but it didn't make it any easier. With more people came more responsibility. Neither Belle nor Lola needed a salary, so there were many months where they'd gone without one in order to continue to grow the business. Lola had her trust fund to fall back on, and Belle had Smith's bank account. Adding employees felt a little like willingly putting themselves in shackles. They'd be responsible for other people's welfare. Not to mention that Belle trusted Lola. That wasn't always an easy dynamic to achieve.

Lola sighed, sensing she was getting nowhere, and gathered her sleek, brunette hair into a pony tail. "I'm going to go grab curry. You want any?"

Before Belle could respond, the door to their studio office opened. There was only one person who had a key to this office besides her and Lola. Belle didn't even have to see him before her body responded. Her nipples beaded tightly beneath her cashmere sweater and she grew damp between her legs.

Lola cast a mischievous glance at her. "On second thought, I think I'll take an actual lunch break today."

Smith grinned as he stepped into the room. Clearly, he had overheard her.

"Take an extra long lunch," he advised.

Belle shifted in her seat at the sight of her husband. He never ceased to have this effect on her. With his dark hair that glinted in the light and the stubble on his jaw line, he could have been a model instead of a lawyer. The weather in London was particularly chilly, and his black cashmere coat hugged his body perfectly. He'd turned the collar up against the wind, and Belle could barely see the knot of his tie peeking behind the buttons. She'd always had a particular fondness for his ties, mostly because he often used them for devious purposes that led to hours of pleasure.

"I'll see you two later," Lola said knowingly. She was smiling as she left, but Belle thought she caught a hint of jealousy on her pretty face. Maybe Lola Bishop wasn't as opposed to finding love as she pretended.

"Do you have any friends?" Belle mused out loud. Even after being married for the better part of a year, she'd only met a few of Smith's acquaintances.

Smith gave a low laugh that sent a tremble racing through her. "I have terrible taste in friends, remember?"

"On second thought, forget I asked," she said.

"Are you planning to play matchmaker?" He glanced over his shoulder at the door Lola had just exited. Was she really so transparent? Maybe her husband simply knew her that well.

"I guess I get sentimental this time of the year." She didn't have to explain herself. They were about to celebrate the second of their two wedding anniversaries. True, they'd only been married for a year, but they had been married twice. They had eloped in November and been remarried with their family and friends by their side last New Year's Eve. One anniversary was legal and the other personal. Still, she couldn't bear not to celebrate both as each meant so much to her.

"I think Lola's not going to have a hard time finding men who are interested," Smith said as he slipped his coat off his broad shoulders and placed it on a hook by the door.

It hung like a streak of black contrast against the white walls. They'd kept the office of Bless purposefully clean and modern. Belle had insisted that the showcase be on the clothes. Now they had had to start renting out a warehouse, but they still had several racks of samples available for their high-end clientèle, the kind they might cater to in person.

To her surprise, Smith continued undressing, removing his suit jacket. She could spot the broad coils of his muscles through his linen shirtsleeves.

"What are you doing here anyway?" she asked, not bothering to squash the hopefulness in her voice.

"I thought I'd grab some lunch," he responded.

"Is that an invitation?" She leaned forward, knowing that her low-cut jumper would put her breasts on display for his enjoyment. His eyes swept down to take them in appreciatively, and then he prowled forward until he was lording over her. With only the desk between them, she'd begun to wonder what pleasure was in store.

"Actually," he explained, "I was trying to decide what I was in the mood for. Curry didn't sound good. Italian? Not what I wanted. As it turns out, there's only one thing I had an appetite for."

Belle ran her tongue over her dry lips to wet them. The discussion had her mind focused on his mouth.

"Then I realized what I wanted," he continued as he circled the desk. Holding out his hands, he waited for her to take them.

Belle knew what it meant to place herself under Smith's

control. She craved it, and now was no exception. He helped her to her feet and then immediately swept her into his arms. Lowering her to the desk, he shoved her sweater up to reveal her breasts.

"No bra, beautiful?" He dipped his head to catch her nipple in his mouth. A moan escaped her as he sucked hungrily. When he released it, the pert mounds were swollen and heavy. "Do you like it when the air hits your tits? You like that, don't you? Because you're dirty."

She breathed a yes, and he rewarded her by paying homage to her other breast. Smith knew exactly how to elicit a response from her. As such, she spent most of the time, even when they were apart, humming with want. He'd been right about why she hadn't worn a bra. Part of her was trained to keep her lingerie to a minimum. If Smith caught her without her bra or knickers, he rewarded her. But she also needed the contact. The sensation of the soft knit brushing against her nipples satisfied some of her need until she could have him.

"This was exactly what I needed," he growled, trailing from the valley between her breasts downward. He hooked his thumbs in the waistband and yanked her pants off along with her knickers. "I needed to devour you."

There was nothing gentle about the way he buried his tongue between her slick seam. Belle cried out as it flicked across her aching clit. Her hands shot out, searching for purchase. She held on as he delved deeper. It wasn't enough though. She arched up, wanting more of him. His arms caught her around the waist and pushed her down.

Belle groaned in frustration and kicked her legs over his shoulders. If he wanted complete control, he should have tied her up. Smith nipped the sensitive nub of her clit in response. It was enough to send her over the edge. Her thighs clamped around his head, trying to push him away and hold him close at the same time. When it became too much, she pulled at his hair, but the suction on her engorged bud increased. He wasn't satisfied.

He never knows when to stop. It was the only thought she could process. Her body fought against the overwhelming sensations as they crowded through her. But with each wild spasm, he took her closer to the brink again. This time when she reached it, pleasure quaked through her and she cried out, completely overcome. When Belle was finally able to open her eyes, she found Smith grinning between her legs.

"I'm stuck," he informed her. That's when she realized her hands were still clenching his hair in a vice grip.

"Sorry," she murmured hazily as she willed her fingers to loosen. It took a concerted effort with her body fighting her. He'd unmoored her, setting her adrift in a chaotic sea, and her mind wanted the assurance of an anchor. As soon as he was freed, Smith took the seat behind the desk. Then he scooped her onto his lap and held her close.

This is one of the perks of being your own boss, she thought. If she wanted to spend the afternoon being fucked by her husband on top of her workspace, there would be no human resources department to fire her. Once they hired more employees, her rendezvouses with Smith would have to wait. She frowned at the unwelcome thought. Lola always knew exactly when to hightail it out of the office. Perhaps, she would get lucky and the new staff members would have a similar sense of self-preservation. If not, Bless might have to find a new home where Belle could have an office with doors.

"What are you thinking about, beautiful?" Smith's husky voice called her from her thoughts.

"The future," she whispered, her words colored with happiness.

"Like round two?" he asked.

"Slightly farther than that," she said dryly. If she only thought that far ahead, she'd never get anything done.

"That far? I hope I'm part of the vision." There was an earnestness to the statement that surprised her.

"Forever," she promised him. Her fingers were still trembling as she brushed her palm down his cheek. There had been dark moments when she thought she might lose him. Those memories were still too raw for her, so whenever he made any mention of what the future might hold she felt an overwhelming possessiveness take hold of her.

She'd never expected to find true love. Not after her first serious relationship had ended in betrayal. Maybe that was how she had found him: by not looking. However Smith Price had come into her life, she had no plans to give him up. They had been through a lot together. More than most couples faced in a lifetime. Some of it she had been able to put behind her. Other things she would carry with her always. Her solace was that he would be there to help her carry the burden. He nuzzled against her, his whiskers tickling her skin, and she giggled.

"You smell like me," she informed him.

"That is my favorite cologne, beautiful." He licked his lips to drive the point home. "Priceless."

"I think it's full of Price actually. Namely my price." She pointed down.

"Rather mine, I think," he corrected. Slanting his head, he kissed her deeply. His lips tasted of the heady mix of arousal and climax he'd drawn from her body. When she was younger, she would never have allowed a man to kiss her after that. But somehow Smith made the forbidden erotic. It was why she could never say no to him.

Still, if she wanted to get any work done, she'd have to start by cutting him off. Wriggling off his lap, she darted out of his reach and collected her trousers. Smith shook his head with disapproval.

"I think I have some mints in the drawer," she told him, giving him a swift kiss on the cheek and wrinkling her nose.

"I like smelling like you," he reminded her. "I'll enjoy it all day and it will give me all sorts of ideas on what I should do to you tonight."

"Don't you have a meeting? Your clients might take offense." Part of her thrilled at the idea of marking her husband with her scent, but the other part didn't relish the idea of him running around London smelling like sex.

"You're no fun, beautiful. Are they in here?"

She glanced over to see him pulling open the left drawer.

"No, not there," she said in a hurry, but it was too late. He was already rifling through it. Then he stopped, his hand on something and his expression unreadable before he pulled a thin compact out of the drawer.

"What's this?" he asked quietly.

He already knew the answer. It was written in disapproval across his handsome face. Belle tried to think of an explanation that would appease him. She could lie and pretend that she had no idea that they were in there, but he wasn't a stupid man. Plus, she'd tried to stop him from looking. She could say they were old, but it didn't matter. Her silence had already spoken volumes.

Smith collapsed into the desk chair, his shoulders drooping under the weight of disappointment. She'd never seen him like this. It was a quiet anger that rolled off of him. Usually he let his feelings be known in a much more vocal manner. The silence between them grew deafening until she couldn't stop herself from filling it.

"I don't know why," she blurted out in answer to a question he hadn't asked.

"So they are birth control pills," he clarified, as he tossed them onto the desktop. "All these months, I thought that you or that I ..."

Smith trailed away. He had never seemed terribly disappointed when her period arrived each month. After their miscarriage the previous winter, they'd halfheartedly agreed to let nature take its course, but when Belle's doctor had offered her the prescription during her follow-up exam, she'd taken it and filled it.

"If you didn't want to have a baby, you could've told me." Accusation sliced through his words. Apparently, she'd been terribly wrong about his desires. How could she have misread him?

"I d-d-do want to have a baby," she stammered. Didn't she? She hadn't been prepared to have this conversation, but now she knew she'd been avoiding the subject entirely.

"It sure as hell doesn't seem like it." He stood and strode across the room, grabbing his jacket from the hook and tugging it on.

When he reached for his coat, she couldn't stop herself. "I didn't think you wanted to have a baby. I thought you were just trying to make me feel better."

He drew it on before turning to face her slowly. "Birds of a feather, remember? I want to have everything with you, Belle. I thought that was a desire that we shared. Maybe I was wrong."

Then he was gone.

CHAPTER THREE

The study was quiet. He hadn't bothered to turn on any lights. Since he'd given up drinking, he didn't need to see to pour a glass. Instead, all he had to do was find a chair. Smith had driven around for a few hours trying to clear his head. When he got home, he half-expected to find her there, but the house was empty. It felt a lot like a metaphor for his life right now. How could she have lied to him for so long? He knew it was more complicated than that, but that was the crux of the issue for him.

When Belle had told him she was unexpectedly pregnant, something he'd never predicted happened. He fell in love with the future, and that destiny had been taken from him only hours later. At the time, he chalked it up to tragedy. There'd been plenty of reason to wait then and plenty of drama to distract him. Once things had calmed down and the two had begun to enjoy their honeymoon together, the tantalizing prospect of that future reappeared. The last few months had been spent in bed, chasing it. Or so he had thought.

He'd seen how happy she was when she told him she was pregnant. There had been apprehension, of course. Since it hadn't been planned, she'd had no idea how he would react, but he'd wanted that baby from that moment. It had been real to both of them, and as each month passed and her period came, life felt a little bleaker. It was a combination of factors, really. He'd wondered if something was wrong with him. That was rational. Somewhere deeper inside him, though, in an ugly place that he tried to ignore, he questioned if he was being punished for his past mistakes. He hated himself every time he couldn't give Belle a child, convinced it was his sins that kept him from completing their family.

Now, he'd discovered it had all been a charade. He was angry with her even though he didn't want to be. In truth, they really hadn't discussed having a child, and he'd made certain assumptions. Logic told him that this was about a lot more than not being ready or miscommunication, still, he couldn't quite see pass the betrayal. He'd been trying to give her the world, and she was rejecting his offer.

"Don't be an arse, Price," he commanded himself. His wife was a much more complicated woman than he was giving her credit for, and she had to have her reasons. But knowing that did nothing to dissipate the sting of it.

The door to the office cracked open, and a slant of light fell across the floor. Belle tiptoed into the room as if she was afraid of him. He didn't really know what to say to her, so he waited. She cleared her throat, and then she took the package of pills out of her purse and tossed them in the rubbish bin.

"I'm not going to take these," she told him.

Smith let his head fall backward in frustration. Somehow he'd managed to guilt her into doing something she didn't want to do. "Take them, don't take them. It's up to you."

"It's up to us," she said softly. "All those things I told you earlier were true, but there's something I left out." She nearly tripped over her own feet trying to take a chair. His hand reached up and flipped on the lamp so that she could see better. That's when he realized she was shaking. She looked delicate cast in the shadows with her pale hair framing her lovely face. His wife had a petite body that drove him crazy. Most of the time she wore heels with black dresses and scarlet lipstick, but right now, she was still in her low-cut sweater and trousers. Her eyes were rimmed red as though she'd been crying.

Smith knew she was strong, but he also knew she could be fragile. As she sat across from him looking small and scared, he felt his anger begin to soften.

"The truth is," she continued in a low voice, "I'm the one who lost the baby. It's my fault."

"It's no one's fault," he cut in.

She shook her head adamantly. "It was my body. I'm the one that's broken."

"We saw the doctor," he reminded her trying to sound gentle. Instantly, her confession had erased all the rage he'd

felt. Now, all he could do was comfort her. How his beautiful, brilliant wife could blame herself for something so far
out of her control, he didn't understand, but he wouldn't
allow her to do so.

"And we didn't get any answers," she said.

Smith thought about rattling off the statistics the
doctor had shared with them. One in four pregnancies
ended in a miscarriage they were told, but that didn't seem
to be the salve she needed. Her wounds ran deeper than he
realized. The only things that could heal her were patience
and love. Getting up, he went to her and dropped to his
knees beside her. Looking into her eyes, he decided not to
offer cursory rationalizations. Not when he had also been
victim to his own paranoia. Hadn't he been the one to
believe for months that they'd been unable to get pregnant
because of his past indiscretions? Was that any more
ridiculous than Belle's fear that her body didn't work? No.
The problem had been that they had not been on the same
page. He took her hands. "Beautiful, there are a million
reasons that we might have lost that baby."

"I don't know if I can go through that again," she whispered. "It still hurts. How can it hurt to miss someone I
never got to know?"

"It hurts me, too," he admitted to her.

"What if it happens again?" she asked.

"Then, it will hurt more," he answered, "but if we don't
try, then we'll never know. And if we don't try, we'll miss
out on the possibility. Even though it hurts now, I fell in
love with the idea of our child, and I got to have that if only

for a few hours. I wouldn't change any of it. You are the best thing that ever happened to me, and I want to share everything with you."

They stared into each other's eyes for a long while. When Belle finally opened her mouth to speak, the trembling was gone. Instead her voice was clear and certain. "I want to have your baby."

Perhaps she didn't mean immediately, but he wasn't going to wait. He stood and reached for her. Their eyes remained locked together as she got to her feet. Sweeping her into his arms, he carried her to the bedroom. This afternoon had been the time for foreplay. Tonight was about connection. When he placed her on the ground, she loosened his tie and tossed it to the ground. There would be no need for that—all they needed was one another. Flesh and bone, body and soul. She fumbled with his buttons and he cupped her face in his hands. He needed to touch her. That wasn't anything new, but the physical urge to feel her skin consumed him. Even the innocent gesture sent a concentrated blast of blood to his dick. It hardened painfully as if it, too, felt the overwhelming compulsion to mate. Belle finished unbuttoning his shirt and slid it off, then she found his cock with her hand.

"No need to rush, beautiful," he murmured.

"I need you inside me," she whispered. "I don't think I've ever needed anything so badly."

He could take his time and still meet her needs, he decided. Moving quickly, he stripped her clothes as she unbuckled his trousers. Within moments they were bared to each other. No matter how many times he saw her body, he would never get enough. The idea that it might change in the coming months—that it might swell and bloom with life—overtook him. Before she could respond, he'd hitched her around his waist and plunged inside her. He didn't care about allowing her time to adjust to his girth. He didn't worry about being rough. Smith knew that the only thing that mattered to either of them was completing one another. Belle cried out as she sank completely onto him. She rocked against him, and he guided her open further. She whimpered as her clit found the friction she sought. He felt it against his skin, proof that she was just as aroused by forging into the unknown as he was.

"Fill me," she pleaded with him.

Oh God, he wanted nothing more. Since the moment he'd seen her, he had known he would never be satisfied until she was dripping with him every waking moment. It was an impossible feat, but he was up to the challenge. Now that impulse was even more undeniable. He carried her to the wall, using it to brace her body as he thrust. His hips pistoned in deep strokes that bumped against her cervix. Belle began to gasp as her muscles clamped around his shaft.

"Harder!"

"Everything for you," he grunted as a sweat broke across his forehead. Somehow this gorgeous creature had chosen him. She had allowed his body to claim hers, and he would never stop giving her everything she deserved. He ground violently against her until her cries rent the air and her pussy milked jet after jet of his seed. Belle collapsed against him, sagging like a limp doll, and he caught her. She clung to him as he took her to the bed, but when he laid her down, she whimpered.

"More," she begged.

Smith stroked his hand down his slick cock, pumping it vigorously as he lowered his body onto hers. Her thighs opened in welcome and he slid inside her in a swift motion that stole her breath. Bracing his palms on the bed, so he wouldn't crush her under his weight, he called to her in a soft voice, "Open your eyes, beautiful."

Belle's lashes fluttered as she struggled to obey his command. She peered up at him through hooded eyelids and murmured dreamily, "Yes, Sir."

"Not tonight," he told her, even though he felt a pang in his balls at her words. She was giving everything to him— her trust, her submission, even her future. His mouth found hers and they kissed languidly, gasping and panting as their bodies moved in a slow, primal rhythm. He lifted his head to marvel at the unbroken circle of their love. "Do you feel that? I'm inside you—giving you life."

She surged around him and he filled her, completing the circle once more.

CHAPTER FOUR

Snow had arrived unseasonably early in London. The delicate flakes grew larger as I watched out the window of my private office. It was yet another reminder that the holidays were only a few weeks away. So was the memo reminding me that we were set to leave for the family home in Balmoral in a little less than a fortnight. And then there was the miniature Christmas tree that a staff member, in their infinite wisdom, had decorated and placed in the corner. The addition would delight Elizabeth when she came to visit Daddy. But no matter what changed, the room still felt like my father's office. In due time, I'd replace the heavy, velvet drapery and send the ostentatious furniture to storage. It was merely a matter of priority. Removing the remnants of my father was less important after we'd been forced to move into Buckingham only a few weeks after the coronation. It didn't feel like home. Perhaps, the holidays would finally change that.

There was a knock on the door and a stammering, young woman peeked in. I rarely noticed the girls on my staff, my eyes completely stuck on my own wife, but I couldn't help but note that the poor thing was practically the shade of a telephone box. That meant that Brexton had arrived for our meeting.

"Show him in." I saved her the humiliation of having to speak.

She nodded and backed up against the door. Her eyes trailed after my old friend as he entered. I'd seen this reaction to him before, even Clara hadn't been immune to his looks the first time they had met. I couldn't be sure if it was the strict, but confident posture he'd developed in the service or the wicked glint of trouble that was omnipresent in his eyes. He was dressed down for the day in jeans and an untucked t-shirt. Judging from the way her eyes lingered it didn't matter if he was wearing this or his uniform as she was preoccupied with undressing him with her eyes.

"Thank you," I called to her as he settled into the chair across from my desk. It took her far too long to realize she'd been dismissed. Curtsying, she quickly shut the door in embarrassment.

"Some things never change," I muttered.

Brexton shrugged as though he had no clue what I was talking about. "Things do change. We used to be out there on the prowl together. Now you don't need a wingman."

"Thank god for that," I said in flat voice. "You were a terrible wingman."

"I resent that. We always went home with a girl," he said.

"You always went home with a girl—usually the one I was eying."

He ran a hand over his closely cropped hair that he still wore in military fashion. "Good thing I was deployed when you met Clara."

I shot him a warning look. Ribbing was one thing. Bringing my wife into it was another.

"What couldn't wait until tomorrow?" he asked, shifting topics before he got into trouble.

"I want you to look into the matter of my father's other son."

"Why?" he asked. It was clear he already knew about the discovery, given how nonplussed he was by my announcement.

"Because it's your job."

He blinked. Brexton Miles had known me far too long to be impressed by my title or authority. Most of the time I appreciated this fact, but today I was immune to the effects of sentimentality. That didn't mean that my good-natured friend and former comrade would simply bow to my will.

Brex relaxed in his seat. Out of uniform he looked like he spent his days in the gym lifting weights, and, no doubt to his tight, black t-shirt, his nights guarding access to night clubs. However, I knew that he'd achieved his formidable physique by carefully adhering to the fitness regime of the Royal Air Force. "Going to boss me around, Poor Boy? I thought we had an understanding."

Despite myself I grinned at the reference to our days on the war front. Brex had treated me no differently then, save to mock my lineage with his tongue-in-cheek nickname. We'd agreed that for him to work on private security team now that our relationship shouldn't change.

"I am your king," I reminded him.

"Bullshit," he called, crossing his arms. "You wanted someone who wouldn't pander to you, remember?"

"I remember," I said in a measured tone. That particular detail had seemed like a good idea at the time. Now I couldn't recall what I had been thinking.

"It was always going to be easier said than done," Brex pointed out. "But that doesn't mean that you are off the hook."

Though I might be inclined to try, I couldn't actually argue with his logic. I needed to switch tactics.

"We don't know where an investigation like this might lead," I explained. "It's possible that this could be connected to my father's assassination."

I swallowed on that final word. Even after a year and a half it was still unfathomable that he had been taken in such a violent manner. Finding out that he had a secret son could be a mere skeleton in the closet or it could be more.

"It seems unlikely—if you want me to be honest." He tacked on the last bit as an afterthought.

"I do want you to be honest," I assured him, "even when I don't like it. But how can we be certain if we don't look into it?"

"We can't," Brex said, "but I suspect the matter of this...

discovery is more about curiosity than it is a matter of national security."

"We can't rule it out. Not without knowing more." My gut told me that I was right about this. None of the secrets my father kept were innocent. "He paid the mother of his love child to keep quiet."

"And he was still paying her at the time of her death," Brex reminded me gently. "Look, I'm not telling you to not look into this, but don't divest all your resources. There were other interesting pieces of information in the files the Americans gave us. We need to examine all of it."

"I need someone I trust looking into this. If you're right and this brother is a nobody, his anonymity will be short-lived if the press find out about him." There had been plenty of speculation regarding my father's romantic life after my mother's untimely death. Even the insinuation of this affair would fuel a tabloid frenzy. Until I knew more about why he'd kept this secret I needed to protect it from the outside world.

"If I focus on this, you'll need to put someone else in charge of the assassination investigation."

That wouldn't be a problem. "A temporary shift in focus shouldn't be a problem since we haven't had any new leads in—"

Brex cut me off, "As I mentioned, the CIA gave us some new information to consider. We've been following an important lead."

"That I haven't been informed of?" I roared as the friendliness I usually felt toward Brexton slipped.

"I considered it prudent to look into the matter further before I briefed you—for the sake of Parliament."

"Parliament?" I repeated. Could he be implying that the conspiracy had its roots in our very government? Judging from the placid detachment in Brexton's eyes that was exactly what he was doing. As soldiers, we'd been taught to compartmentalize. By keeping our emotions in check we wouldn't make decisions based on our feelings. Brex still had that ability. I did not.

For the first time, I allowed my control over the room to falter. Dropping my head into my hands, I considered the position I found myself in now. Neither avenue of investigation could be dismissed outright. Both need to be examined—thoroughly and by people I trusted.

"Could Norris?" Brexton suggested as though he could sense my dilemma.

I shook my head, finally lifting it to meet his gaze. "He's in charge of Clara and Elizabeth."

No matter how my situation might change or what information became available, they had to remain my primary concern. No answers and no justice were worth putting the two of them at risk. Clara still ruffled at my security measures, but she'd grown accustomed to Norris's presence. But not only was it a matter of my wife's happiness, it also came down to the fact that he was the only person I trusted with the two people I loved most in the world.

"In that case, that only leaves one other person." We both knew who he was talking about, but there was no missing his hesitation. It wasn't a suggestion he would make lightly given my history.

"You trust her?" I asked. The number of people in a position to take over Brexton's work was limited. That meant that I needed to delegate some of the decisions to him. But even so it was a tough pill to swallow.

"I do. I know the two of you had some issues in the past."

I raised an eyebrow as I tried to decipher what he was really saying. If he knew the true nature of my relationship with his colleague or if he'd merely guessed. I didn't have many secrets from my friend, but I didn't discuss Georgia Kincaid if I could help it.

"She's discreet." It was the most complimentary trait I could find to describe her. Georgia had once helped initiate me into the world of Dominance. As far as I knew she didn't brag that I'd been a past client nor did she share the other men of power she'd submitted to. Our relationship had never been sexual but rather a therapeutic proposition. I'd realized far too late that it had been a power play on behalf of her employer to keep me under his thumb. "But she's also a mercenary. Her loyalty can be bought."

Brexton's shoulders tensed, a vein ticking in his neck, at my words. Even so he was remarkably calm as he responded. "She was a mercenary. She's proven her loyalty to our side."

I bit my tongue before I could ask when he had fallen in love with her. His attachments were none of my business, and Brexton was smart enough to handle her if she proved to still be trouble. I should have seen the inevitability of the romance, but I'd been too caught up in my own affairs to redirect his attention.

"I suppose people change," I offered. I had changed with Clara's help.

"Yes, they do." There was a finality in his tone that even I didn't dare question. "It's your call."

It was my choice. Every possible decision had its disadvantages, but none of them outweighed the danger of inaction. "Brief her."

Brexton nodded, maintaining a professional detachment at my proclamation, but I spotted a gleam of triumph in his eyes. He stood, straightening as if he might salute me. Thinking better of it, he headed for the door.

"Brex," I called before he could leave my office, "tread carefully."

The triumph faded but he managed a much curter nod of acknowledgment.

He might not like to hear it, but it was my responsibility as a friend to warn him. Perhaps my past associations with Georgia had left me prejudiced against her. Still despite our differences, I was certain of one thing: no one ever really knew Georgia.

Except one person.

I was dialing his mobile before my conscious thoughts caught up with my body. Smith answered on the third ring.

"Yes?" The subtle trace of Scot in his tone only underscored his obvious disregard for my position. Then again, an alpha male never bowed to another alpha male, regardless of title.

"My hand has been forced." I explained the situation, taking care to leave out why I'd reassigned Brexton. If Smith was curious about what other matter I found more pressing, he didn't ask. "Keep an eye on Georgia."

"Is that an order?" he asked dryly.

It was a very good thing that we were having this conversation over the phone. The man knew how to get under my skin. We'd achieved a tenuous peace over the last year, but our relationship remained strained at the best times. Like now. I had to remind myself that he was my ally.

"I like to think of it as a mutually beneficial request." When it came to the safety of those we loved, Smith and I saw eye to eye. I was counting on that understanding now.

There was a pause. "Consider it done."

CHAPTER FIVE

"**A**re you planning to leave your study this evening?"

I startled at the sound of my wife's voice. Tearing myself away from the file I'd been reading for the fifth time, I glanced up. Clara paused in the doorway, the light from the hall cast a glowing silhouette around her. It framed her like an angel, and that's what she was: my own angel sent to deliver me from myself. She stepped forward and came into better view. Her dark hair fell over her shoulders and her face was fresh, free of any cosmetics. She wore a simple white, silk robe that skimmed along her divine body. As I drank her in, the points of her breasts beaded under the thin fabric. I loved how her body responded to me, even at this distance.

"What time is it?" I asked, rubbing the back of my neck absently. What I was really asking was how long I had to fuck her before she pleaded for sleep. If it was up to me, I'd spend every moment of my life making love to her.

Her eyebrow arched as a smile twisted over her face. She knew exactly what I was thinking. "It's ten. Bedtime."

"Would you like me to join you?" I reached for the power button on my computer monitor. She didn't have much of a choice as to whether I joined her if she was going to walk around looking so tempting.

"If isn't too much trouble." She sauntered to the desk and bent over, tapping her fingers on the mahogany. Bending slightly forward, her robe fluttered open enough to reveal a glimpse of creamy breast. "Unless you have something better to do."

"Tonight I'm taking what's mine, poppet." If she wasn't careful, I'd be claiming her on the top of this desk. But as I stood my mobile vibrated in my pocket. I shot her an apologetic smile and she shrugged. She had grown accustomed to quick messages and late night crises. Once I had her naked nothing short of nuclear war would be enough to draw my attention away from her. Slipping the phone from my trousers, I checked the screen. I couldn't stop myself from grimacing when I saw the text from Brexton, and without thinking, I dropped back into my chair. Georgia had gleefully agreed to take the new assignment. That didn't surprise me, but I wasn't thrilled to have her heading up such an important matter.

"What's wrong?" Clara asked, studying my features.

"Nothing," I lied, and my wife frowned. The two of us had been through far too much for me to get something past her. She knew my moods, mercurial as they were, and she loved me anyway. But she had no patience for lies. I shot off a quick response, reminding myself that sometimes the less she knew, the less she had to worry about. Clara might disagree with that assessment but I considered it a marital duty.

Clara came around the desk and carefully climbed onto my lap. Judging from the heat between her legs, the robe was all she was wearing. I couldn't help but enjoy the sensation of her cunt nuzzling against my groin. She pressed a finger to my chin and drew my face up to hers to plant a soft, inviting kiss on my lips.

"Tell me what's on your mind." Apparently her invitation came with a price.

"Nothing you should worry about." This time I wasn't lying. Instead I tried to be reassuring. There was no need for Clara to carry my burdens. She'd given up a normal life by marrying me and I wouldn't pile every matter of state or security on her. "Only one of us should be tasked with dealing with the mundane issues of the country."

"That's not it." Her eyes searched mine for the answer that wasn't forthcoming. "This isn't some Parliamentary issue. You've been preoccupied since we left the States. Talk to me about it. I can help."

"Just being with you helps." It did. Her presence was a comforting assurance that I was acting of her best interest.

"I don't like it when you keep things from me, X," she warned.

I brushed a kiss over her mouth, and she sighed. Her

47

body softened against me despite her hesitance. "Sometimes you have to trust me."

"I could say the same thing." Clara buried her face into my shoulder. "I can handle it. Whatever it is. We said no secrets, remember?"

We had. I promised her that I was through keeping secrets from her, and then I'd proceeded to keep them anyway. Not because I didn't trust her, but because I loved her. If only she could see that. I had to make her understand. "My only concern is with protecting you."

Clara stayed silent and I could see her struggling with how to respond. I suspected the reason I'd gotten away with my past indiscretions had a lot to do with her knowing exactly why I had made the choices I did. Her life had been threatened on more than one occasion. It was a fact that I couldn't live with.

"I'm stronger than you think," she said at last. "I can handle it."

"If you only knew." I laughed under my breath. "If you had any idea how much I struggle with my need to protect you."

"Show me. Let me in. Take what you need from me." She stroked her hand down the side of my face.

It was an offer that I found difficult to refuse. Since the moment I'd met Clara, I'd felt compelled to watch over her. But not simply to just protect her. I wanted to claim her— own her. I'd longed to take that lovely creature and spirit her away where I would be the only one to ever touch her. She would be safe with me, and she would be mine. I tore my gaze from her and the temptation she was unknowingly dangling over me. "You don't know what you're saying."

She caught my face and held it steady. "I am yours. All of me. Take what you need, and nothing less."

"Clara." I swallowed against the longing building inside me. I had to put a stop to this. "I could never."

"You can. I'm asking you to. Whatever it takes. I don't want anything between us. Show me."

Her words vanquished my resistance, and I slid my arms around her. Lifting her into my arms as I stood, I carried her toward our bedroom. Clara exhaled contentedly as I laid her across our bed and plucked open the sash of her robe. It fell open to reveal the luscious curves of her body. I took a step back and surveyed my prize. On another night I would take her right then and there. My cock throbbed as if to second this plan, but I ignored it. I always needed her body. I always wanted it. Tonight, I demanded her freedom.

"Take it off," I commanded her.

Clara wriggled under my watchful gaze until she shrugged the robe from her shoulders. Reaching down, I slid it free from her until it was only her, stripped to nothing for me. She waited, her breath speeding up with expectation. When I moved away from the bed, she remained still. Clara enjoyed it when we played, so when I went to the closet, she made no effort to stop me. At the far end of the walk-in an antique armoire waited ominously. I kept the key with me at all times in an effort to prevent a curious maid from discovering its contents. Opening the black lacquer door, I found what I was looking for immediately. I chose the white, silk rope because it seemed fitting given that I had deprived Clara of her robe. While I loved the sight of red bindings on my wife's fair skin, tonight I wanted the innocence. Despite my tastes, there was a purity to Clara that even my darkness couldn't touch.

I reappeared over her with the rope and surprise flashed over her eyes. Perhaps she thought this was a game. Or a test. I saw it for what it was—for what she had given me. An offering. At times, she forgot what I was. I would remind her of that. I was the predator.

Clara held out her wrists, crossed in supplication. I uncrossed them, meeting her eyes as I took one firmly. She didn't pull away as my grip tightened. This part I would do slowly if only to grant her a second chance. I kept my gaze locked to hers and wondered if she saw the darkness of my thoughts. Leaning down, I found her ankle and urged her leg up. She bent it willingly, even as I brought her wrist to her calf. Then I began to work, looping and tucking until her arm and leg were tied tightly to one another. I repeated the action on the other side. When I was done her legs were spread and bound, displaying the pretty pink gash of her cunt. Her knees pressed into the soft mounds of her breasts, her nipples peeking from above. I wanted to take them in my mouth and suck until she came, but this wasn't about pleasure. She licked her lips, her eyes hooding with want.

"This is what I want, poppet," I murmured. I drew my hand through the air over her naked sex, just enough to stir the air so that she would squirm against her restraints. "I want you helpless to my control. I want to tie you up and lock you away."

"X," she whispered, her eyes widening as she began to piece together what I was saying.

"Shh," I hushed her. "I want you to be mine. I want you to do as I say. Right now you'll do anything I ask, won't you?"

She swallowed, managing to move her head enough for a slight nod.

"All I want is to know that you're here." I didn't wait for my words to sink in before I turned and left her there. Shutting the bedroom door behind me, I walked back to my study and poured myself a bourbon. It should make me feel like a monster for leaving her like that, but instead I took pleasure in it. Some of the weight I'd carried with me since we met had lifted from my shoulders. I took my responsibility for Clara seriously. Since I'd accidentally dragged her into my life, I'd worried for her safety every moment she wasn't in my sight. I was a modern enough man to know that I couldn't reasonably expect my wife to be near me at all times. Even when we were home, her absence from presence needled me. Now there was no question what she was doing or who she was with. I had never known real freedom in my life , and I hated that I savored taking hers now.

I sipped my drink slowly. It burned down my throat.

Clara was a wild thing that allowed me to tame her at her pleasure. I had pushed her past her comfort levels before. In every case, she had asked it of me. But that didn't mean she understood when I crossed the line. I had no idea what to expect when I went back to her this evening. She had told me to take what I needed from her, and I had done it. Too often people in my life offered me lip service without devotion. My wife served my pleasure in my bed and I always rewarded her trust. But there had always been the promise of limits coloring our intimacy. I'd abandoned that. Draining the last of my glass, I stood and left it on the table. I paused and listened at the door. No sound came from within. I opened it a crack and caught sight of her on the bed. I had no idea if it had been minutes or hours. I only knew that enough time had passed to call me back to her. My heart pounded in my chest and I strode toward her.

She didn't speak when I reached her. Her eyes were closed but I spotted two dried trails of tears. I undid my cuff links as I waited. She didn't open her eyes. I left them on the nightstand and began to undo the buttons on my shirt. I'd taken off all of my clothes before her lashes fluttered. When our eyes met, they were full—of tears, of accusations, of need.

"I'm here now," I said in a soft voice. There was no way to be sure she would find that comforting, but it was all I had to offer. I took a step closer, careful not touch her. "You know what to say."

Given the hurt shining in her eyes, I knew she needed

to be reminded that one word would stop all of this., When her mouth opened she said something I didn't expect. "Please."

My fists clenched into balls as the request processed. My hand dropped to cup the mound of her sex and she moaned. I felt my balls constrict at the sensation of wet heat. Clara tried to push against my touch as if she was desperate for more, but I wouldn't take her this way. I'd always rewarded her trust and tonight would be no exception. Stooping, I undid her bindings and took care to rub the indentations the rope had left in her soft flesh. When she was free and I had massaged away any lingering discomfort, I helped her into a sitting position. Seating myself beside her, I waited. She moved like her limbs were foreign objects until slowly she lowered her body onto my lap. I drew her legs around my waist, encouraging my dick to sink deeper. Clara's breath caught as I impaled her and she released it with a strangled cry as I took her hips and gently rocked her. She stared at me, her expression unreadable, and as we climbed together, she brought her hands to my face to trace the curves of my jawline and my brow. Then she kissed me deeply. She was my air and I released her hips, clutching her body to mine. I would never let her go. I couldn't.

"I love you," I groaned when the kiss broke. Clara's eyes stayed trained on mine, and as I felt the first spasm of pleasure grip my cock, I saw sadness wash over her. We rode out our climax together, but I refused to relinquish her when the waves subsided. She pulled against my hold and I loosened my grip, but only enough to allow her to draw back. She slapped me with a force that vibrated across my cheek.

Shoving me to the mattress, she extricated her body from mine and backed away. "Don't ever touch me again."

"Clara." I sat up, alarmed. Every ounce of me wanted to go to her and hold her while she raged and sobbed. Whatever it would take, I would give—just as she'd given me my darkest fantasy. But I stayed still. Right now the best thing I could do was listen and hear what she was saying. "Clara, I—"

"Don't bother," she advised me, her voice rich with warning. "I asked for it, didn't I? So that made it okay?"

I opened my mouth to speak, but she held up a hand.

"Leave."

If there was ever any question that she was a queen, that command laid it to rest. She lorded over me, too far to touch as I got to my feet. I hesitated and turned to her, but she looked past me as if she couldn't see me. Or perhaps, and the thought left a sick dread in its wake, as if she didn't want to.

I bent and collected my pants from the floor. Sliding them on, I tried to buy myself more time with her. Maybe the more willing I was to meet her demands, the sooner she would unleash the full force of her fury. I didn't look forward to that, but facing the storm would be better than remaining in purgatory. When I slid the buckle of my belt into place, she was still pointing at the door. I guessed I had my answer. I collected my shirt and left the room, shutting the door behind me. A few moments later I heard the lock click in place.

"Good job," I told myself. I couldn't help but feel torn. Had I really expected a different outcome? My eyes clenched shut and before I realized what I was doing, my fist slammed into the wall. The ancient plaster cracked but didn't give way.

Why had she let me touch her if she was that angry? She had every opportunity to use her safe word. Instead she had asked me to touch her. I didn't know what it meant but my heart sank into my stomach.

Penny, the nursemaid, came around the corner and stopped dead in her tracks. She gawked at my half-clothed body and I felt my anger rise to the surface.

"Don't you have somewhere to be," I barked.

The poor girl jumped a little, then scurried away. I could only imagine the rumors that would be circulating amongst the staff in a matter of hours. Wadding my shirt in my hands, I stalked back to the bottle of bourbon I'd left behind.

After an hour, I checked our bedroom door and found it unlocked. I peeked behind it, but the room was empty. The only sign of occupancy were the wrinkles we'd left behind on the damask bed spread. The fireplace was unlit and that fact, combined with Clara's absence from our bedroom, left the space cold and lifeless. If my wife wasn't enjoying the few hours of sleep she could expect before Elizabeth woke us in the night, then she was fuming. I didn't dare think of it as sulking or pouting. She had a right to her anger. What I'd done was inexcusable, even by my standards and since I had no plans to apologize, I knew I shouldn't expect a reprieve. We might find ourselves well into the new year before she forgave me.

Abandoning the empty bedroom, I sought her in the only other place she ever frequented in the short time we had lived here. I'd made certain that the Queen's Sitting Room was updated for her use as soon as I learned that we must move. My grandmother had been the last person to use the parlour regularly and I knew Clara would appreciate neither her decorating or feeling as if she was under the former Queen Mother's thumb. Grandmother had removed herself to Sandringham shortly after the coronation, so none of us would have to keep up the pretenses of civility.

I'd asked the staff to make the room feel light and airy, wanting to give Clara a place that felt entirely different than the rest of our palatial home. It was impossible to cover up the gilded carvings around the room, but they'd been minimized by sheer curtains that allowed sunlight to stream into the room. Now at night ribbons of moonlight slanted across the furniture inside. Clara was tucked into a ball on one, staring out the window into the starless night. I cleared my throat to warn her of my entrance, but she didn't bother to look to me.

"Poppet," I tested the waters with my pet name. Still no response. I debated my options. If I continued to call out to her, it was likely she would continue to ignore me. If I went to her, I could expect a physical response. She'd never had control over her body in my presence. However, given what I'd put her through, it felt wrong to rely on such provocation.

"Are you going to stand there and muse all night?" she said softly, her eyes directed away from me.

The fact that she was talking to me seemed a good sign, but I didn't miss how she kept her body turned from me. It was a message. I crossed an important boundary. Throughout our relationship, I had been the one to insist on precautions to protect her from my unpredictable nature. What was worse that I had disregarded my own rules or that I didn't feel sorry for them?

"Clara, I…" I trailed away, unsure what I should say.

"Don't apologize," she demanded.

"I wasn't going to," I told her softly. Despite her command, she turned a furious gaze on me. It wouldn't be the first time a woman said one thing when she felt entirely the opposite. I'm not certain what it said about the male sex that it still surprised us.

"You should!" she exploded, wrapping her arms tightly around her knees and clutching them to her body.

"You're giving me mixed signals, poppet." It was the wrong thing to say. I knew the moment it left my mouth, and now I would suffer the consequences of two verbal slip-ups.

"I am?" she asked in disbelief, her blue eyes flashing darkly. "I'm giving you mixed signals. Well, Your Majesty, you have a convenient habit of choosing which of your own rules you want to follow."

"I deserve that." But the admission wasn't going to appease her.

"For example, you were the one who insisted that we have a safe word," she continued, "but you have to be in the same goddamn room to know if I'm going to use it."

"You weren't in danger," I reminded her gently. "Be rational."

"Don't you ever tell a woman who's tied up and alone to rationalize her situation. You promised to protect me."

Admittedly her accusation stung. But that was what she didn't understand. I had been protecting her. If I could only make her understand. First, I would have to get a word in edgewise.

"You're also supposed to respect me," she said.

"Clara," I cut her off sharply. There was a time and place for feelings, but I could no longer allow her to misinterpret my actions. "I do respect you."

"Like hell you do."

"I respect you and I was protecting you." I kept going in an attempt to explain myself before she ran away from me. "Will you let me explain?"

"You can try." Her words sliced through the air but her chin dropped to rest on her knees. She was granting me an audience, but I knew I only had one chance to get this right.

"You offered me anything I needed from you." I paused and waited for her to confirm this. All I got was a begrudging tilt of her head. "So, I took what I needed."

"Bravo," she interjected. "That really clears things up."

I had expected that response. I didn't relish how long it might take for her to see the situation through my eyes. "You know that I struggle with my compulsions. You've lived through the bodyguards and the distance and—"

"And the stalking?" she suggested.

I felt a twitch of annoyance in my jaw, but I ignored it. "Since that night in Brimstone I have wanted to take you and lock you away. I've wanted to keep you from the world, so they could never hurt you. I understand that's not the politically correct way to have a relationship." I attempted a small smile but it was met with a glare.

"That's not the sane way to have a relationship, X."

Using my nickname? I decided to take it as another good sign. "I resisted my urges then and focused on less mental ways of protecting you. I know you hate the bodyguards and security sweeps."

"They're part of being with you," she said, "and I accepted that. But if you're going to tell me that you need to lock me away to satisfy your compulsions, then you can kindly go and fuck yourself."

"I don't need that," I reassured her.

"Then what was that?" she cried out. Our eyes met and I saw the moisture pooling near the edges. She blinked, but the tears didn't dissipate. "I told you to take what you needed. I want to give you want you need, but I don't know if I can give you that."

"I don't need you to." I was repeating myself, although I knew it wouldn't reassure her. "I took advantage of your offer."

"You took advantage of my submission," she whispered.

"I was always going to push your boundaries." I felt sick saying it. I thought I'd become a better man for her. Now I realized I was still as fucked up as ever.

"And there will be no apologies for that," she said.

I shook my head. "I took what you gave freely."

Clara stood in a rush, her eyes darting between me and the door. I knew she was calculating whether she could get around me. When she stayed frozen in place, I guessed that she decided she couldn't. That left her with pushing my boundaries: would I be able to let her go? Would I come after her?

History proved I would, and we both knew it.

"Clara, I don't want you to be angry with me."

She laughed mirthlessly and tightened the sash of her robe with a quick yank. "It's a bit late for that. If you wanted to be in my good graces you could have just tied me up and fucked me. I thought we were past this controlling bullshit."

The string of profanities littering her responses told me that she had only gotten more frustrated with me.

"I wish I could be the man you deserve," I admit.

"I do, too." Her words were a slap in the face, but she didn't back down. "But you are the man I want—the man that I chose. That doesn't absolve you from what you did, though. When are you going to see that I'm here with you? You aren't going to scare me away, X. Not if you give me yourself. But you might push me away if you keep taking me without letting me in."

"I want your life to be full of happiness." Not stress or fear. I didn't want to burden my beautiful wife with the secrets that continued to crash down upon me.

"How can it be when you keep resurrecting walls between us?" The softness of her words only made them fall heavier. "I know that we aren't like most couples. You have to guide a country. I can't run out to the market. So much of our lives have been determined for us."

"For that I am sorry." I'd tried to let Clara go when we first met, because I knew that claiming her would only bind her to a life of responsibility.

"I chose that life," she reminded me, taking a tentative step in my direction before she stopped again. If we were too close to one another, we'd fall back on bad habits and wind up in each other's arms. "But the duty should never affect us. There are no security precautions or state secrets. There can't be. You know that."

"Most of what I deal with would bore you," I assured her with a wink.

"Don't you dare!" She pointed a finger at me. "Don't pretend like it's all boring, mundane action items. You are keeping something from me. You have been since we were in DC."

"Clara, I only want to—"

"Protect me?" she guessed with a sigh. "You aren't. You're protecting yourself. Maybe you think I'll be angry or maybe you don't really trust me. Honestly, trying to figure out why you keep secrets is exhausting. I didn't marry you to have secrets between us."

"I won't ask you to carry them."

"Don't you see?" she asked in a weary voice. "You don't have a choice. We're in this together. I can't imagine telling you that I don't need your help."

"You do all the time," I said dryly.

"But you're still there, helping me," she corrected. "It's what we do. Distance doesn't work for us. We might as well try to be abstinent. It will go over about as well as you keep secrets. You don't have to carry your burdens alone, and I don't want you to. That's what I was offering you tonight. All of me. You want to protect me, but when will you see that I want to protect you?"

It took all my resolve not to gather her in my arms and carry her to our bed. I'd overstepped a line tonight and I wouldn't take advantage of her vulnerability in this moment. Especially given that I couldn't tell her what she asked of me. "Some secrets aren't mine to share."

"Then there's our problem. All of me is yours to share." A sob wrenched from her and she shook her head. "At least, it was."

"Clara, please—" I couldn't stop myself from reaching for her then.

"Don't!" She pulled back. "Not tonight. I'll get over it. I'll learn to live with it. Tonight, I need to be alone with the truth."

"What truth?" I dared to ask, even though I didn't want to know.

"That I let myself be swept into the fairytale," she murmured. "I fell under your spell. I let myself believe in happily ever after. I swallowed a pretty story because I fell in love."

"It isn't a fairy tale. This is real." I moved toward her, but she darted past me. "Clara, we're real."

She paused at the door and turned sad eyes on me. "Maybe we were."

CHAPTER SIX

SCOTLAND

The tree would never do. It had been delivered from the village earlier this week, and there were far too many scraggly patches that revealed its crooked brown limbs. No amount of ornaments or decorations could hide that fact. On the off chance that his grandmother decided to join them for the holidays this year, she would send it back immediately, but that wasn't what concerned him. This Christmas had to be perfect. The family had eschewed tradition last year and stayed in London for the holidays. Elizabeth was still a newborn and there had been the chaos surrounding Belle and Smith—knocking off to Scotland hadn't been a priority. That meant this was David's first year celebrating with him at Balmoral, and since Edward hadn't given him a wedding yet, he could give him a proper Christmas morning.

That was easier said than done, given how hard David was pushing back against his preparations.

Strong arms wrapped around his waist as he studied the tree, and he felt David's chin drop to his shoulder. "It's fine."

"It's ugly. What will Belle and Clara say?" He knew David had a soft spot for his best friends, and he wasn't above using it to his advantage.

"They'll be too busy worshiping their husbands to notice," he promised.

David had a point, but Edward didn't miss the edge to his words. Both Clara and Belle had husbands to command their attention; David did not. Maybe he was less obsessed with the perfect Christmas as he was with distracting him from that fact. He hadn't been able to explain to David why he'd continued to push back their wedding date. Just as David didn't know nearly enough about the events that transpired a year ago. Edward had kept the secret out of respect for his friends, but also under the command of his brother.

"I thought we came earlier to be alone," David said pointedly.

"We are alone," he snapped, and David pulled away.

"Alone together, not separately. I can't help but think you've dragged the whole of England's problems with us."

Maybe he had. Edward had brought the Royal Family's problems at least.

"You've been distracted." David stepped closer, frustration blazing in his eyes. "I've been understanding, but you can't keep avoiding your own life."

"I know that you—"

"This isn't about me," David interrupted. "I'm not making threats or ultimatums. Although Christ knows that I should be. I'm simply pointing out that you're only hurting yourself."

They both knew that wasn't true. "And you."

"All things considered, you've come out of the closet, declared your love for me, and upset hundreds of years of tradition just by proposing to me. I shouldn't expect any more miracles in such a short time frame."

"I was the one who proposed," Edward pointed out. He'd made a promise when he asked David to marry him. He didn't take that lightly, but he'd done it when he had no idea about the threat looming over his family. It was possible that whoever was behind the attacks on his brother and father had only been after Alexander. Edward had almost convinced himself as such until Belle had fallen in love with the wrong man. Smith Price, now her husband, had proved his love for her but the secrets he'd revealed had shown that Alexander's paranoia had been warranted. Most of this had been kept from David. In truth, Edward knew very little. His brother hadn't been eager to share his information with anyone. Despite everything, Alexander still believed it was his role to martyr himself for the sake of his family. What bits of information Edward was privy to didn't paint a clear picture. Edward had proposed in good faith and that faith had been slowly stripped away over the last year.

"Yes," David said, drawing his attention back to him, "and if you've changed your mind…"

It took a second for Edward to process what he was saying, but then realization dawned on him. David thought this was about him. How could Edward reassure him otherwise when he couldn't tell him the truth? Alexander had commanded secrecy, and since he wasn't sharing news of the investigation with his own wife, he couldn't breach his trust. "This isn't about you. Or us. It's—"

"Then marry me," David cut him short.

"I will," he promised, but David shook his head.

"Now."

"But the wedding and…"

"Everyone will be here for Christmas. Everyone we care about, and if your brother doesn't have the authority to marry us, no one does. I don't need a big wedding, I just need you."

Edward's heart melted a little at the sincerity shining in his brown eyes. He'd made this man wait for him to be ready for years. "I want to, but there are laws."

"Sod the laws."

"I am the Prince of England," Edward reminded him dryly. If something happened to Alexander, the throne would have to pass to him until Elizabeth came of age. He had to consider his place and responsibility.

"You will always be the Prince of England." There was an implication in David's words that Edward didn't want to consider. "That's not going to change. If you feel that you can't be both Prince and my husband, then maybe it would be best if..."

David absently twisted the ring on his finger, and Edward's heart twisted along with it. Was this really what it would come down to? Choosing between the man he loved and the legacy he'd been born to? It occurred to him that this was how Alexander must have felt when he fell in love with Clara. Although the two had faced scrutiny, scandal, and danger, they'd continued to choose each other. Why couldn't he do the same?

"Yes," Edward said.

"Yes?" David repeated questioningly.

"Yes, I will marry you." Grabbing him by the shirt, Edward drew him roughly to his body. Their mouths crushed together, the air around them charged with an electricity that he'd only felt in his arms. He had shielded himself from it in recent months, trying to keep him safe from unknown enemies by putting distance between them. Now Edward knew he'd only been hurting them by doing that. The love he felt for him transmuted into an intense longing that grew as the kiss deepened. Loosening his grip on him, Edward's hand slipped lower until he found the hardening bulge through David's jeans. David moaned against his mouth as he began to stroke through the thick denim.

The two had always given and taken, each a generous lover, but today Edward wanted to erase any doubts. The idea that David had ever questioned his love wrecked him, and he felt compelled to show his love exactly how much he loved him. Breaking away, he met David's chocolate eyes for a moment before dropping to his knees. Only a selfless act would be enough to show him, even though he took an immense pleasure in performing it. His fingers slid David's zipper down nimbly, and in one practiced motion, Edward freed his cock from the confines of his shorts. It fell heavy and hot into his hands, and Edward began to caress his length as he brought its broad crown to his lips. His mouth closed over the tip, allowing his tongue to swirl languidly until he swallowed it deeply into his throat. David groaned, his hands fisting in Edwards hair as he continued to suck.

"That feels so fucking good," David grunted as he began to rock against Edward's mouth.

They fell into a rhythm and Edward felt his own dick begin to ache. He couldn't stop himself from shoving his hand down his trousers to stroke it as he continued to pleasure his lover.

"It turns you on to have my cock in your mouth, doesn't it?" David growled.

Edward nodded, taking David deeper. He responded by thrusting harder, his balls slapping against his chin, as he fucked his throat. Edward felt the first clench of his own balls, even as he nearly gagged on David's length, and when the first, hot jet shot against his throat, his own release broke free and coated his palm. He licked his shaft as he released him, and David sighed with pleasure.

"My turn?" David asked huskily as he helped Edward to his feet. Edward grinned sheepishly.

"I might have already..." he trailed away as David spotted his sticky hand.

"I don't mind a challenge," David promised him before he crushed his lips to his. When he broke away, they were both panting and rock hard. "Maybe we should take this show to the bedroom before Mrs. Watson comes in and has a heart attack, though."

Edward chuckled at the thought. Balmoral's house-keeper had been in tenure since he was a boy. She was a grumpy, old hen who complained about everything from her arthritic hip to the quality of the village's clotted cream. She had welcomed David with open arms, but she was getting up there in years. The two had already decided that all of this Christmas's house guests needed a gentle reminder not to let her catch them doing anything too shocking. Although it might be easier to lock the fragile Mrs. Watson in her quarters instead of relying on the discretion of any of the couples.

"Lead the way," Edward encouraged him, and David took his hand.

It was beginning to look a lot like Christmas.

CHAPTER SEVEN

$\mathcal{I}$n Smith's experience, a phone call from Georgia Kincaid never meant good news. The woman's presence in his life could be most easily described with comparisons to natural disasters. Like hurricanes and tornadoes, she was an inevitability that could not be avoided. No matter how prepared you were.

Smith bypassed valet parking. It was a service he only used in the presence of Belle, whom he wouldn't dare make walk more than a few feet into a building. When he had the option, he generally preferred to keep other hands off the steering wheel of his Bugatti. Even as a grown man, he didn't like to share his toys. He found a particularly secluded spot marked no parking, pulled in and got out of the car. His mobile would alert him if any wanker tried to tow it. That seemed unlikely given the close quarters of London garages and between his smile and his wallet, he could have a boot taken off in no time.

The Westminster Royal hotel was known for ensuring the privacy of its guests. He paused at the revolving door and nodded in greeting to the bell man as he adjusted his tie. Another married man might think twice about meeting a woman, who wasn't his wife in a hotel, but if Belle found out that he had done so, her first concern wouldn't be with the fact that he was meeting up with Georgia. She would never suspect an affair. Instead, she'd interrogate him as to what intelligence he'd gathered. In that regard, he had a united front with his wife. He'd kept her in the loop as much as possible once he'd realized she was the first person in his life he could trust. At times, it had been necessary to keep her in the dark, but she'd always understood that. Still, he preferred to not bother her with any information unless it proved to be of vital importance.

The small bar off the hotel's lobby was relatively busy for a weekday afternoon, but with Christmas only a few days away, more people were taking off work to see to their final holiday shopping. On one hand, this meant their conversation was more likely to be overheard. On the other, it was far more likely that everyone here would be too preoccupied with their own chaotic to-do lists to eavesdrop. He didn't have to look hard once he stepped inside the bar area.

Even with her back turned to him, Georgia stood out in the crowd. Long, black hair swung well past her shoulders and judging from how she flipped it with a toss of her head, she was in the midst of a flirtation. It was the seductive combination of Georgia's looks and her charm that made doors open for her. It was also what had made her a formidable assassin once. Those days were behind her now. Like Smith, she'd chosen to go legit when it became clear that their mutual employer was mixed up in a political game that could destroy them all. Smith had acted based on conscience, but he didn't dare believe that Georgia had acted out of anything other than self-interest. Her beauty may have gotten her behind locked doors, but her survival skills had kept her alive on more than one occasion.

He strode toward her and waited until she finished flirting with the bartender. She paused, winking at Smith so quickly that he almost wondered if he'd imagined it.

"I'm sorry, I have to take this to go," she told the other man, nearly sounding as if she meant it. Smith knew better. Picking up her rocks glass, she tilted her head to a table in the corner.

"That's lucky," Smith said dryly. Given how busy the bar was, it couldn't have been chance that secured a perfect location for a clandestine meeting.

"I rely on many things in my life," Georgia told him. "Luck isn't one of them."

He gestured for her to step in front of him, never mind the fact that Georgia Kincaid was as far from a lady as a woman got. Chivalry must observed. As she sashayed toward the table on four-inch stiletto heels, he noted her strength and confidence. After the attack that had nearly claimed her life a year ago, he'd wondered if she would change. Some things were different now. She had a new job and respectable connections, and, as far as he knew, she'd given up certain unsavory side employment along with her new life. It didn't feel prudent to ask her. Still, despite the veneer of self-confidence, he knew the truth. Smith had seen the scars. He'd read the medical report. Abortions. Suicide attempts. No one would guess the darkness that shadowed her life by looking at her. Georgia's past was as big of a contradiction as she was herself. One moment, she was the most commanding presence he'd ever seen and in the next, she was begging to be dominated. In public she ruled, and in private she submitted, and the face she wore, even to those who knew her best, only hid the pain of her past.

She took the seat against the wall. It was a wise choice. She could see everyone in the room that way, he thought, but it left him to take the chair with the partially obscured view. Georgia always had the high ground. She was always protecting herself.

"So, what's going on?" Smith asked as soon as they were seated.

She swirled the amber liquid in the bottom of her glass and shrugged. "Can't an old friend call someone for drinks? It is Christmas time."

"I had no idea you'd developed a sentimental streak," he said.

A waiter appeared at the table and took his drink order. Georgia raised an eyebrow as soon as he disappeared. "A club soda? Are you pregnant?"

Annoyance shot through him. She had no way to know

what a sensitive subject she'd broached, but he gave her a tight smile. "Everyone changes, I don't need to tell you that."

In truth, he hadn't discussed his recent sobriety with anyone. Belle had noticed, but kept her mouth shut. During his time employed by Hammond, he'd reached all too often for the bottle. It had been a habit of his father's as well. Now that he was attempting to be a better man, drying up seemed like a good idea. He didn't feel the need to explain this to Georgia, and she didn't press him on it. That was why their relationship worked.

"I've been given a new assignment. One that I think you'll find interesting." She tapped her fingernail on her own glass.

"I thought you were going professional these days," he said, tipping his head in thanks as the waiter delivered his club soda. "I'm not on the Crown's payroll."

Was this why Alexander had asked him to keep an eye on her? Did he suspect she would share classified intelligence as soon as she saw it? He'd agreed to do so because Alexander had insinuated that it affected the safety of his wife. He, like Belle, wanted to be in the loop. After working for Hammond he understood the importance of knowing gossip before it became fact. Still, he couldn't stomach being dragged back into the affair. If Georgia was no longer on the right side of the law, he wasn't certain he wanted to know. It would force him to choose between his longtime allegiance to her and his promise to Alexander.

"I'm still a good girl—for the most part. But given the

importance of this topic to the both of us, I felt it under-standable to share."

He froze, his glass midway to his mouth. There was only one shared interest that would send Georgia calling upon him.

"I'm out," he reminded her. The night that Hammond had died, Smith had gone to kill him himself. Instead, he had walked away after Hammond had delivered a pardon to his adopted son. He had informed Smith that they were all pawns in a much larger game, but since Hammond had been burned, Smith was off the hook. All he had to do to ensure his own safety, and his wife's, was to mind his own business, and he had for the last year. Now both Alexander and Georgia were trying to drag him into the fray once more.

"No one's ever really out," Georgia murmured.

"I am." Smith's voice was firm. Getting involved in whatever she was investigating would only lead the wolves back to his door. He'd have to speak with Alexander and make his wishes clear. He respected the man's compulsion to protect his wife, but now Alexander would have to respect his desire to do the same. He wouldn't risk Belle to protect Clara.

"You don't care then about the people we lost—about everything we gave up?" she asked. Incredulity was not an emotion that she wore often. It looked as out of place as if she had shown up in a rainbow jumper and pigtails.

"Why are you surprised?" he asked. "I only ever wanted to get out. I wanted my life to be my own. It is now."

"They tried to kill you and your wife," she reminded him.

"Hammond tried to kill my wife," he told her. There have been no more attempts on Belle's life since the last time he spoken with the dead man. That was proof enough to Smith that the threat had died with him. "I'm not interested in revenge."

"Suit yourself." She drained the rest of her drink and placed her empty glass back on the table. "I'll continue to look into this."

She had always had a much stronger need for revenge than Smith but she'd also faced horrors he hadn't. Whatever ghost drove her to pursue revenge were her own to appease. Still he was curious, even if he didn't plan to take action. He had always wondered who was been behind Hammond and his anti-Royal conspiracy. It had been a shock to find out that his ex-employer wasn't the one pulling the strings. The true mastermind had stayed in the shadows, hiding himself so well that this was the first time Georgia had seemed genuinely optimistic in a lead.

He couldn't help but bite. "So, once you have him, will it be the Crown's justice or your own?"

A coy smile snaked across her lips. "I haven't decided yet."

"You'll get yourself fired." *Or worse*, he thought to himself. Then again, there were those in high places who might feel inclined to help her out in a pinch—if for no other reason then to protect their own anonymity. If she ever decided to sing the tragic aria of her past, Smith knew there'd be more than a few well-known names included in that melody. "I pity the man when you find out who he is."

"Oh, I already know." She fluttered her lashes, looking anything save innocent.

Leave it to Georgia to drop that bombshell after he'd already sworn his neutrality. Asking for a name couldn't hurt. Could it? The chances that it was anyone Smith knew seemed unlikely, and given she was half the people he cared about in this world—or even spoke to for that matter —he predicted no feelings of betrayal.

"You're dying to know, aren't you?" she guessed when he remained silent.

"It won't change anything," he assured her. He'd made his choice. It was up to Alexander and his men now to concern themselves with this matter. So long as Smith and Belle were of no interest, he held none of his own. "It won't matter."

"Somehow I think it will," she said.

He took a long sip of his club soda, wishing, not for the first time, that it had a higher alcohol content. Or for that matter, any alcohol content. He kept this thought to himself.

"Who is it?" he asked at last.

"We're waiting for confirmation," she prefaced.

He shook his head. She was just teasing him now. She'd gotten him to ask and she wanted to enjoy making him wait. Whatever information they had was enough to catch Georgia's interest. He knew she didn't act rashly, which meant the evidence was damning.

"Who?" he repeated, uninterested in continuing her cat and mouse game.

"Some rising star in Parliament," she said.

"Why would that concern me?" Smith had never been particularly interested in politics. It was a useless fascination that distracted far too many intelligent men. Bureaucracy was a tool for those who preferred red-tape to productivity. "I probably couldn't name a single member of Parliament."

"That's what I thought when I first heard," she said, "but as I learned more about him, I found the connection."

"What connection?" he asked slowly. She hadn't called *him* on a whim. That much he knew. If he was sitting here it was because she had information that would catch his attention.

"He recently bought an estate. Seems he's trying to gentrify himself. We've had a few analysts profile him in an effort to see if he's capable of what we think he's capable of. I didn't need to wait for their reports. I've seen him. He is."

The prickle at the back of his neck told him what she hadn't yet. It filtered into his veins, turning his blood to ice while he waited for the final nail.

"His name is Oliver Jacobson," she continued. "I can't be certain, but given that he's your mother-in-law's new neighbor, I thought you two might have met."

Smith swallowed on the lump forming in his throat, but it had lodged in place. He didn't need her to tell him more. For the most part the man was a stranger. Smith had only spent a few hours in his presence. It had been Belle that

Jacobson rubbed the wrong way. At the time, Smith chalked up his wife's dislike of the man to maternal difficulties. Jacobson had made himself useful to Belle's mother. He'd been visiting the Stuart family home for months before the Prices had sought refuge there. The few discomforting moments he'd had with the man, Smith had written off as the subsequent effects of his wife's paranoia. But now things began to click into place: the offhand remarks about the privileged aristocracy, the chilling moment Jacobson had held a gun far too close to Smith's head for comfort, and, of course, Jacobson's interest in the Stuart family.

Belle hadn't walked into Smith's life on accident. She had been sent, and Smith had been given the task of grooming her to be a source of information. His wife was meant to be an unwitting spy on her best friend and the Royal family. But by then Smith had already betrayed Hammond and those behind the conspiracy he was embroiled in. It couldn't be a coincidence that Oliver Jacobson was so well-acquainted with the Stuarts.

When the waiter reappeared and Georgia ordered two bourbons, Smith didn't object. She folded her hands on the table and waited as he processed what she had revealed to him. There was no need to speak. She didn't need to say *I told you so*, although she was barely holding back a smirk.

Georgia had been right. She'd known all along that this would change everything. Smith could no longer stay neutral. The enemy was far too close to home.

CHAPTER EIGHT

*H*arrods was packed with hundreds of last minute shoppers. It was all Clara could do to keep track of Belle amid the chaos. Their annual Christmas shopping trip had been a tradition since their days in university. Planning it these days was a little trickier than it used to be. It had taken Clara a fair bit of psychological gymnastics to convince Norris, her personal security guard, that she could go somewhere so crowded and public in the weeks leading up to the holidays.

Who was she kidding? These days it took considerable guilt trips for her to leave the palace grounds outside of diplomatic duties. She'd agreed to go in a way that would neither draw attention nor jeopardize her safety. That meant she'd been forced to wear a Burberry scarf around her head. Given how rarely she'd been photographed wearing anything but dresses and heels, she'd opted for

Armani jeans and nude flats. She wasn't just shopping with
Belle though. Norris was nearby. She couldn't see him. He
blended into the crowd too well. She doubted that a
woman at the perfume counter could get a spritz off a
bottle before he'd be there pulling her to safety.

"Are you sure you don't want sunglasses?" Belle said
dryly as they paused at a scarf display. She reached up and
fiddled with the fringe on Clara's cashmere scarf.

"Don't remind me how ridiculous I look," Clara
pleaded. This was as close as life got to normal for her.
She'd have to settle for it. Right now, she needed to pretend
that she was just another woman out for a day with her
best friend. Otherwise, she'd be forced to think of the situation at home.

Clara had always been hesitant to share her relationship
problems with Belle. Alexander was a private man. Every
glimpse he afforded her into his own guarded interior was
too precious for her to divulge. She'd have to settle for
being out and away.

"Is everything okay?" Belle asked, as if she sensed how
preoccupied Clara had become.

"Fine," she said absently. Belle's lips pursed. She didn't
believe her, but she also didn't push it any further. Clara
considered for a moment. "We're fighting," she admitted.

She didn't really have to say anything more. Belle was a
married woman herself now. Given that she'd married a
lawyer, she was probably no stranger to arguments herself.

"Anything serious?" Belle asked. She was choosing her

words carefully, which Clara was grateful for. It was a tactic the two had become accustomed to in recent months. Clara didn't particularly like how the dynamic in their relationship had shifted. Though it had been inevitable, when Belle became involved with Smith Price. She'd begun to keep as many secrets as Alexander, even choosing not to tell Clara when she eloped in New York. They'd managed to both look past their hurt feelings. That was, after all, what best friends did, but nothing had been quite the same since.

"Just the usual," Clara told her. "He's being overprotective and unreasonable. You'd think he was the King of England or something."

Belle giggled appreciatively. "Smith isn't much better, and he doesn't have a title to hide behind."

"I can't stand it," Clara confessed. She wandered over to a display of holiday tea and sniffed the sample. It seemed like an appropriately safe present for her own mother. "I hate the security guards and the constant scrutiny. I hate feeling like a prisoner in my own home."

She left it at that. Belle didn't need to know that her husband had tied her up and left her for an hour in the bedroom. Alexander's proclivities behind closed doors was a subject Clara was fiercely protective of. Plus, she wouldn't put it past her best friend to beat down Alexander's door and let him have it.

Belle remained silent, and Clara realized she had struck a nerve.

"I like it," her best friend finally admitted. "Ever since what happened with Smith, I don't mind that we have a security team. I don't even notice them most of the time, and it makes me feel better."

Clara couldn't help but wonder when the two of them had switched places. Once, Clara had been vulnerable, afraid of her own shadow. It had been a product of the abusive relationship between her and her ex-boyfriend, Daniel. Despite the increased interest in her personal life, she'd railed against Alexander's obsessive need to know where she was, what she was doing, and that she was safe. In all fairness, he had every reason to be concerned, but Clara was determined to remain her own person, even though she'd taken on a life of public service.

Belle had been the wild card at university. Despite being engaged during that time, she could vacillate between dutiful and daring within seconds. It had been something Clara admired about her. Now Belle was the one who preferred to isolate herself. It took considerable effort for Clara to get her to go into public. Clara even knew that her own sister, Lola, who joined Belle's startup company had stepped in to takeover most of the public relations. Belle refused to be the public face of Bless. It was as if she wanted to be a ghost.

Clara decided to respect Belle's wishes, even if she didn't understand them.

"Who do you have left to shop for?" Belle asked.

Clara sensed she was changing the topic. She still had to

pick up something for Alexander. Given how angry she was with him, now didn't seem like the best time to buy him a present. He'd done stupid things plenty of times, but for whatever reason, this has crossed a line and she didn't know how to step back over it.

"I need something for Elizabeth," she said, instead. "I know she'll get plenty of things, but I feel like I should get her a special present." Her little princess was already spoiled. She was the first grand baby, the first niece, and the first child. Elizabeth wanted for nothing. Still, Clara had precious few opportunities to purchase something for her child in person.

They headed to the children's department. Elizabeth was petite, taking after neither her mother nor her father, as far as Clara was concerned, so she was still in infant sizes.

"This is darling," Clara cooed, picking up a red velvet cape with a little matching hat. She turned to flash it to Belle but froze when she saw her best friend's face.

Belle was fingering the lacy hem of a christening dress and stopped when she realized Clara was staring.

"I've been thinking about expanding Bless," she explained too hurriedly. "Children grow out of clothes so quickly. At least, that's what I'm told. It might be useful if you didn't have to buy them all."

"Of course," Clara agreed with her. She sensed there was more to this preoccupation than what Belle was sharing. It hadn't occurred to Clara that visiting the children's clothing department might upset her best friend. A considerable amount of time had passed since Belle had confided that she had lost a pregnancy. The subject hadn't come up since. That meant Clara had to make a choice. Belle hadn't pressed for more information when Clara was upset earlier, but that had been an issue of marital difficulty. It seemed that what was on her friend's mind was something that she needed to share.

"Do you want to talk about it?" she asked Belle softly.

Belle began to shake her head, but then thought better of it. She cleared her throat before she began to speak. When she finally did, her words were thick with emotion. "You know I had a miscarriage" Belle began, her words thick with emotion, "It was right after Smith and I were married. It wasn't planned. I didn't mean to get pregnant. So much was going on, I'm not even sure how it happened. I barely had time to process the fact that I was going to have a baby before it was taken away from me. It seems like so much was taken away from me last year."

Clara searched for the right question to ask. She knew a thing or two about unplanned pregnancies, but unlike Belle, she hadn't lost a baby. To know her best friend had been silently carrying this pain for so long broke her heart.

"I know it's been a year," Belle continued, "and I should be over it."

"Love doesn't run on clocks," Clara murmured, recalling the wise words Norris had once shared with her. "I think you get to be sad for as long as you need to be."

"Even if it's forever?" Belle whispered.

"Even then," Clara assured her. She paused. She had already forced her best friend to own up to what was bothering her. Now she had to decide if she should pursue the painful subject. "Are you trying to have a baby?"

"Yes," Belle said after some hesitation, "and no."

"I think that's what's called a conflicting report," Clara said softly. She gave her best friend an encouraging smile as she re-hung the small velvet cape. Maybe this wasn't the best place to be having this particular conversation.

Over her shoulder, she caught sight of Norris, who was staying safely distant. She guided Belle away from petite reminders of what she lost—and what she still stood to lose. They stopped when they found a children's play table tucked in the corner.

"This isn't terribly dignified," Belle noted as they sat in the miniature chairs.

"Who says I have to be dignified?" Clara asked. The joke cut a little bit of the tension and Belle relaxed.

"I said I wanted to try because it was so obvious to me that Smith did."

"But?" Clara prompted.

"I kept taking my birth control pills anyway," Belle confessed.

"So, you didn't want to have a baby."

"No, I do. That's the strange part. I don't know why I kept taking the pills, except that maybe I was scared."

"No one can blame you for being scared," Clara said

encouragingly. "Not only did you not plan to get pregnant in the first place, then you lost the baby. That's a lot to deal with, especially given everything else you were going through at the time. How do you feel about it now?"

"Better," Belle said. "Smith found the birth control pills and lost his shit. I had no idea it was so important to him to have a baby."

"Men are funny that way," Clara said in a dry voice. Alexander hadn't had been happy when she found out she was pregnant, but since Elizabeth's birth, she suspected he'd been trying to knock her up every time he took her to bed. She had never quite decided if it was because he adored Elizabeth, which he did, or because he seemed to take pleasure in the proof of his own virility. "Have you talked to him about this?"

"A little." Belle took a deep breath. "I threw away the pills. I told him so. I guess part of me is scared to get pregnant again, but it's not because I don't want to have his baby."

Clara wanted to tell her that everything would be all right, but she knew how damaging a thoughtless, if pretty, lie could be. She wouldn't try to appease her best friend with a platitude. "No matter what happens, I'll be here for you."

It was the only comfort she could offer. Belle smiled gratefully. Apparently, it would be enough.

"Come on," she said to Clara, standing up and wiping away the few tears that had managed to escape during their talk. "I need to buy something for Elizabeth, too."

WHEN CLARA'S mobile began to ring, she ignored it. Amid the crush of holiday shoppers it seemed imprudent to try to have a phone conversation. But when it continued to vibrate in her purse, she decided it couldn't be ignored. Given the number of times it had rang in a minute, she expected Alexander's name to be on the missed call log. Instead, she was surprised to see it was Edward. She flashed the screen to Belle, who shook her head.

"Isn't he supposed to be having a romantic moment alone with his fiancé?" she asked.

Clara didn't want to jinx anything by saying what she was thinking, but she suspected there might be trouble in paradise. Edward had been avoiding choosing a new wedding date for far too long since he'd postponed the original date David and him had settled upon. With all the other stresses of the holiday season, she couldn't help but wonder if matters had finally come to a head. The phone began to ring again and Clara looked to Belle. "I think we're done shopping."

She shot off a quick text message to Edward so he'd stop calling her repeatedly, and then began to search around her for Norris. She caught his eye in no time. He stepped forward and they hurried over to him.

"Edward is having some type of psychotic break." Belle explained. "We need to get to the car and call him back."

"As you wish." He clamped his mouth shut before he could add *Your Majesty*. Clara had asked him repeatedly to stop calling her by that moniker, particularly when they were in public, and she thanked him with a smile. It wasn't easy for Norris to ignore matters of etiquette, but he was more like a father figure to both her and Alexander than an employee. He stepped to one side to make a call and a few minutes later, he led them out the front door.

The arrival of a guarded car caught numerous shopper's attentions, and when the wind caught Clara's scarf and blew it away from her face, she knew it was a lost cause. Mobile phones came out and people snapped pictures. Norris hustled her away from the burgeoning crowd. At least, there were no paparazzi around to make the horror complete. No doubt Alexander would be seeing stories about her impromptu shopping trip from any of the number of the Royal blogs that stalked their every movement.

A twisted thrill ran through her at the idea of pissing him off a little. Every once in a while it was good for him not to get his way.

Belle practically shoved her in the back seat before anyone could take more photos, and when they finally settled in, they abandoned their shopping bags, so Clara could dial Edward. He answered before the phone had even rang on their end.

"Are you dying?" Clara asked him in a flat voice.

"I was wondering the same thing," he retorted. It was easy to see through his mock annoyance. Edward was the more charming of the Cambridge brothers. Being the acknowledged spare to the throne and hiding his sexuality for so long, he'd developed a charismatic wit that ensured his survival amongst the modern day court. It was one of the reasons Clara had warmed to him immediately, and when she'd introduced Edward to Belle the three of them had become the closest of friends.

"If you aren't too busy, I have a bit of an emergency," he announced.

"What's wrong?" Clara's attitude immediately shifted to concern.

"You sound like such a mum when you say that," Belle grumbled next to her. "Honestly, you should see her, Edward. You'd think she was going to burst into tears."

"Do shut up." Clara bumped against her shoulder. "He doesn't care about my emotional whims. Why are you calling us every five seconds?"

"If you're busy," Edward suggested, "I can just call someone else."

"Not bloody likely," Belle said. "Spill."

"Well, David and I are here getting everything ready for Christmas and fighting over the tree."

"Naturally." Clara interjected.

"I know, it's terribly gay of us," Edward said, before continuing, "and...I don't know exactly how to say this, but we've decided to get married."

"Tell us something we don't know." Belle said slowly. She looked to Clara with narrowed eyes.

"Like, *now*," Edward clarified. "Or over the holidays."

"You're getting married for Christmas?" Clara clapped a

hand over her mouth. Tears threatened to spill over. She'd never hear the end of it if she started to cry now.

"We were thinking for the New Year."

"That's hardly a distinction," Belle said. "Were you going to tell us? Or were you worried I'd think you were a copy cat."

"I thought if we had the same anniversary, you could make certain I don't cock up and forget a present every year," he informed them. "Besides, you're supposed to be here in a week, and I was kind of hoping you might come early."

"Of course!" Belle and Clara said at the same time.

"There's a lot we need to do," Edward rambled on, as if he hadn't heard them, "And I know you're both busy. Belle you have your business, and Clara you have—"

"We'll be there." Clara interrupted before he could talk himself out of it. If she had the opportunity, she would get her brother-in-law down the aisle. He'd been dragging his feet far too long not for her to jump at the chance to marry him off at long last.

"I'll need to arrange it with Smith," Belle said. "But of course we can come early."

"And Clara will need Alexander's permission." Edward teased.

"No, I won't." Clara said defensively, earning an awkward silence from both of her friends. It stretched across the phone lines until Edward finally broke it.

"Then it's settled. Call me when as you've cleared everything up." As soon as they hung up, Clara threw her arms around Belle in a tight hug, and the two began to laugh.

"You are an emotional roller coaster," she accused.

Clara pulled back, her eyes bright. She'd been dreading spending the holidays cooped up with her unrepentant husband. Instead, she'd be distracted in the best possible way. "I can't help it. It looks like Christmas is coming early this year."

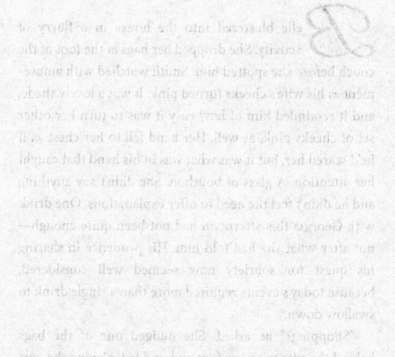

CHAPTER NINE

*B*elle blustered into the house in a flurry of activity. She dropped her bags at the foot of the couch before she spotted him. Smith watched with amusement as his wife's cheeks turned pink. It was a lovely shade, and it reminded him of how easy it was to turn her other set of cheeks pink, as well. Her hand fell to her chest as if he'd scared her, but it was what was in his hand that caught her attention. A glass of bourbon. She didn't say anything and he didn't feel the need to offer explanations. One drink with Georgia this afternoon had not been quite enough—not after what she had told him. His prudence in sharing his quest for sobriety now seemed well considered, because today's events required more than a single drink to swallow down.

"Shopping?" he asked. She nudged one of the bags behind the sofa with her foot and nodded, playing the part of the innocent. "Something for me?"

"Something for me to wear for you," she purred. The innocent act disappeared, replaced by a full-fledged vixen.

"Do I have to wait for Christmas?" Right now nothing sounded better than burying himself deep inside his wife. Judging by the way she sauntered towards him, she had the same idea. But when she crawled onto his lap, she bit her lip. Something was on her mind. "Out with it, beautiful."

Belle didn't have to play coy often. They had money, so she never had to ask to spend it. He was obsessed with her, which meant that damn near everything she requested, he found a way to give her. But he didn't mind being in the position of power at the moment. Power was something he rather liked, especially when he could exercise it over his wife.

She hooked an arm around his neck and nuzzled against his jaw and whispered, "I have a favor to ask."

His dick was growing harder in his pants. She could ask for the moon right now and he'd find a way to lasso it. "Anything."

"I need to leave for Scotland in the morning."

That request was unexpected. Now he understood why she was tantalizing him. He popped a lazy eye open and looked at her. "I can't leave for Scotland in the morning."

She knew that already, which was what had brought on her seduction. Although he'd largely retired from legal work, at her provocation he had decided to take on pro bono work. He had a meeting with a client a few days from now. She kept well-informed on his cases, so she knew when he would be home late.

"But I need to go to Scotland," she continued to brush her lips against his jawline.

While it took considerable effort, he managed to grab her by the hips and break away from her spell. Smith wasn't fond of his wife being apart from him. The thought of her being in another country was unbearable, even if it was a neighboring one. However, after what Georgia had told him this afternoon, perhaps it was a good idea.

She took his hesitation as denial and began to pout. "Edward's decided to elope. You can't tell anyone." She rushed to say, as though Smith was about to get on the phone and call the tabloids.

"I was about to phone the press," he said in a flat voice. She stuck her tongue out at him, which only made her look more adorable. This was exactly how the little blonde vixen on his lap had wormed her way into his heart. She'd been wild and uncontrollable and all too eager to sink to her knees for him. He shifted uncomfortably, trying to ignore the steady uptick of interest in his pants at the thought.

"He wants Clara and I to come and help. Clara has already gotten permission."

That was a lie. Smith knew it. Alexander's obsession with his wife made Smith look like a sensitive twenty-first century male.

"Why do you need to go?" he asked. "Doesn't he have a whole staff who could put this together?"

"Because we're his best friends." Belle explained. "And

we'll need to plan a bachelorette party or a stag night. I'm not really sure which he'd prefer."

"If you think the idea of you running around town, hopping from pub to pub is going to sell me on this idea, beautiful, you're mistaken."

The flirtatiousness slipped from her face and she began to glare. "If you think you can order me to stay home instead of going to celebrate with my best friend before he gets married, then you're mistaken, Sir."

She added the last bit with emphasis.

"I ought to take you over my knee for being so petulant," he warned. "But you'd like that, wouldn't you?" Belle always enjoyed a little fight before her submissive side came out to play.

"Or," she suggested, leaning forward to employ her feminine wiles again, "I could make it worth your while."

"Beautiful, you make everything worth my while," he assured her. Her hand slipped down and found the rock-hard bulge, he was doing his best to ignore. In actuality, she didn't have to work so hard. He had made up his mind, almost as soon as she'd asked. If Smith was going to follow-up on this information from Georgia, it would be better if Belle was safely out of the way. He had no idea whether Jacobson was in London or in his country home. Not for the first time, Smith was relieved that they wouldn't be spending Christmas with Belle's mother and brother on the family estate. He had helped his wife sell her interest in Stuart Hall to her half-brother earlier this year. That was a decision that was paying off in spades, because it meant that Belle felt no inclination to return there. Now that Smith knew Jacobson had been behind the attacks, she wouldn't be allowed to return; not until Jacobson was dealt with. Sending Belle to Scotland, where there were already armed guards, seemed like a smart move.

Belle pressed her index finger to his chin and drew his attention to her. "What's on your mind?"

"How many hours I'll need to fuck you before I'll be able to let you out of my sight," he said gruffly. She believed him because it wasn't a lie. He just left out some of the other important bits. It made him sick to think that the entire time they'd sought sanctuary from Hammond and his men at her family home, that they'd been in danger.

Jacobson had chosen not to act and Smith didn't understand why. He could have killed Smith that day in the forest, returned to Stuart Hall, and finished the job. Mary Stuart had welcomed Jacobson into her home without batting an eye. Smith couldn't help but wonder how much of the politician's decision to buy the adjoining estate had to do with his wife. It was another matter he'd have to look into.

"Seriously, Price," Belle demanded his attention. "You are in la-la land."

"Do you want me to show you what I'm thinking about?" he asked.

"Yes, Sir." She bit her lip again, but this time it was followed by a shy nod. He loved how her eagerness mixed with vulnerability whenever he shared his plans to take her to bed.

"You can go to Scotland," he said in a husky voice.

"And you'll come next week, right?" she asked, her eyes widening.

"Yes," he promised.

But it was a lie. He had no right to make such promises. Not with what he had to do. Despite that, his responsibilities would wait until morning. "Do you want to go to the bedroom, beautiful?"

She nodded again, a little quicker this time.

"Then show me the way."

Belle needed no further encouragement. Sliding from his lap, she found her way to the floor and began to crawl on her hands and knees toward the staircase. Smith watched appreciatively. It wouldn't be the last time tonight that he enjoyed the sight of his wife on all fours. He licked his lips as she paused at the foot of the stairs and popped back onto her heels. She was such a natural submissive—absolutely breathtaking in her willingness to please.

He stood and removed his belt in one swift motion. Walking toward her he slid it through his open palm. She tensed a little, but he knew she was simply preparing. Pain wasn't what Smith needed tonight, even if she might deserve a little spanking for her games. Instead, he looped it loosely around her throat and tugged.

"Come, beautiful," he commanded. Tonight he needed to possess her. He needed to claim her. No matter what happened in the coming days, he would leave Belle Price with no doubt that she belonged to him.

CHAPTER TEN

A week. I'd rarely spent this long outside Clara's good graces save for the dark periods when we were apart—after we'd first met and in the aftermath of my father's assassination. My wife had been angry with me since, and often. This time she was avoiding me. No doubt owing to the number of arranged and political marriages the monarchy had seen in the past, we both had our own bed chambers. It was a technicality since we took residence. I slept with my wife, and I would have it no other way. Since our fight, Clara had locked the door, forcing me to sleep in my own room. Her bedroom—our bedroom— connected with the nursery, so it was fair. But the dismissal meant that I found myself missing both the comfort of her body pressed against mine and waking to care for Elizabeth in the night. Without the nearness of both of my beloveds, I couldn't sleep. As such I'd found myself taking up temporary residence in my office.

Throughout the day, I'd catch myself dozing off in my chair, my naps interrupted by staff members delivering paperwork or afternoon tea.

The more time I spent in the office, the more it felt like it belonged to me rather than my father. It was an unwelcome sensation. I didn't want to belong here. I'd accepted my role as King because it meant I could protect Clara and our children. Without her presence, I'd begun to question if I had become what I'd once hated. Was I my father? A man more obsessed with his own power than his own family?

A fire had been lit in the hearth and its heat warmed the air like a sedative. Abandoning my desk, I took the leather wingback next to it. I was a man who lived for his work. I was a man who bound himself to duty. What further proof did I need but the desire to take a nap in my private study? I clutched the worn, but recently oiled armrests and willed my eyes to open. I stared at the cream, brocade wall-coverings until my irises burned from the effort.

She'd gone shopping this afternoon without telling me. It was a perfectly normal thing for an average wife to do, but Clara was not your average wife. Norris had gone with her, and *he* had told me. I'd been informed, but it didn't change the fact that Clara was living life as she saw fit. Despite the fact that my information came from others, I was receiving her message loud and clear. She would not be ordered about. It would be a wonder if she didn't bring the whole monarchy to a crashing halt on her own. But her going out wasn't what bothered me, it was that she believed she shouldn't tell me. Not only was I concerned that I was becoming my father, now it seemed my wife was, too.

"You can choose the sort of man you become," I said to no one in particular. Even alone, I couldn't bring myself to believe it. It was something Clara might say to me. Would I believe it if she had spoken those words? I closed my eyes and tried to hear them coming from her voice.

A soft knock startled me and I snapped. "Enter."

Norris stepped inside and I relaxed. I couldn't handle the appearance of a timid staffer sent to delivery sandwiches on a silver tray. Not right now. My longtime bodyguard, and if I was being honest the man I considered a true father, didn't look at all ruffled by my tone. He eyed me appraisingly, and although his face betrayed nothing, I knew what he saw. I also knew he disapproved of it.

He looked nothing like what one might imagine a personal security officer looked like. Instead, he looked average with a medium build and a forgettable, if kind, face. In actuality, that made him a formidable presence. It would be unwise to go against him. The last man that had gotten around the security perimeters in place had met his end at Norris's hands. While my old friend considered it a failing that Daniel, Clara's ex-boyfriend, had tricked his way into our wedding, I knew that my wife was alive because Norris had been there that day.

"Might I have a moment?" he asked.

I waved him inside, bracing myself for a lecture. Norris was one of the few men who could get away with chastising a king. Mostly due to the fact that he'd been gently correcting my behavior since I was a child. But also, because I owed Clara's life to him. It was a debt I could never repay given that I held her life in far more regard than my own.

He shut the door behind him before he came to take the seat across from mine. He didn't wait for further permission.

"Please sit," I said dryly. Regardless of his standing within my life, I was in no mood today.

His eyes narrowed at my petulant comment. He took a moment to adjust his cuff links. He would reward my sullen attitude with making me wait even longer for his rebuke.

"Her Majesty plans to depart early for Scotland. She wishes me to pass along the information," he informed me.

"For fuck's sake!" I smashed my fist against the armrest. "Can she tell me nothing herself?"

Norris remained silent, but it was obvious he felt that was answer enough.

I forced myself to regain my composure. "Am I expected to come?"

"I assume that you'll want to discuss that with her, Sir." I didn't miss the insinuation in his words. He was calling me to action. If Clara wouldn't come to speak with me, he would send me to speak with her.

"I doubt it," I grumbled.

"You're not sleeping," he pointed out. There was a time when he would have noticed this much earlier on, but his orders had changed since my marriage. Norris's primary concern was Clara's safety. As Clara refused to be near me, I hadn't seen much of him over the last week.

"I've had a lot on my mind." I folded my hands in my lap. "Why aren't you with Clara?"

"She's in the nursery with your daughter," he said as he settled into his seat. Stroking a hand along his jaw, he studied me for a moment. "In truth, she needs very little by means of protection at the moment. She hasn't left her private chambers for days. She refuses company. And if you will pardon the intrusion of your privacy, she sleeps alone."

"My wife's sleeping arrangements aren't your concern," I bit out. I didn't need a reminder that she was sleeping alone. Not when I was well aware that I was sleeping alone, too.

"Alexander," he said my name firmly. "Do not presume to speak to me like one of the hired help."

"Aren't you?" I asked. But even as I said it, I looked toward the fire.

"I am not." His voice shifted into a softer tone. "I don't need to tell you that. I consider Clara and your child as more than a duty. They are my family, because I think of you as my son."

My eyes flickered to the oil portrait that still hung over the fireplace. Sooner or later I would be forced to replace it with my own. For now, my father looked down at me with disapproval. "Am I as big of a disappointment to you as I was to him?"

"Only when you act like a proper brat," he said. "And you only act that way when you are unhappy in love. Thankfully, that is not very often."

"I regret to inform you then that there is no end in sight to this particular bout of petulance."

"I suspected as much given Clara's behavior."

I wanted to ask him what he meant by that. Had she been crying? Was she still angry? Depressed? I kept the questions to myself. In truth, I thought of Norris as the father I'd chosen rather than the one of my blood. While he knew more about my personal life than most parents might choose, I felt far too possessive of my wife at the moment to share even my thoughts with him.

"I'm not in the mood to discuss my marriage," I warned him.

"That's fine." He shifted in his seat but he didn't rise. "I'll talk. You listen. No discussion."

I might be the King of England but I knew there was no point to refusing him.

"You and Clara have weathered some trying storms since you've met. Often the trouble came from those around you," he began.

It was like a father to overlook my poor behavior when I first met Clara. Norris seemed to sense what I was thinking as he continued.

"You acted in her own interest. I've watched you reject your birthright since you were a child. I know that you wanted to protect her from this life and that you were willing to give her up despite your love for her if it meant giving her the freedom you've never had."

My mouth grew dry and I struggled to maintain my calm. I had tried to give her up. It was what was best for her then, and as Norris spoke, I knew it was what was best for her now. The reality of that realization didn't make it any easier to consider.

"But you can't give her up," he said gently. "Nor can she give you up. You are bound to Clara by more than just a marriage vow. Your souls are bound to one another. Still the two of you fight for control."

"I only want what is best for her," I interjected. How could he accuse me of being power hungry when he knew my true intentions? Norris understood the dangers associated with being a member of this family better than anyone.

"And she you," he said. "But you must learn to give yourself to her."

"I've given myself to her completely." A dangerous anger rippled through me at his insinuation. He should know me better than this, and if he didn't and she didn't, who ever would?

"Have you?" he asked in a soft voice.

"I've given up everything to protect her," I roared. "My freedom. My choices. She is the only thing I care about. Her safety—her life—is my number one concern."

"That is not giving yourself to her. That is giving yourself for her," he corrected me. "A man must open his heart to the woman he loves. He must bare his soul—his scars and his fears."

"Why?" I asked in a defeated voice. "Why must she bear my mistakes? My sins? My burdens?"

"Because she vowed to share your life—your whole life."

"I want her to be happy."

"You make her happy, Alexander." He leaned forward, shaking his head as if annoyed to have to point out something so obvious. "Your troubles cannot take that from her."

"I haven't told her about my other brother," I admitted. "Without knowing more about why he was kept a secret, I don't want to worry her."

"Why do you think it will scare her?" he asked.

"I'm not certain." I searched for a reason for my own fears but I couldn't find it.

"Has she asked you to protect her from worry?"

I shook my head. "She hates it when I keep what's bothering me to myself."

"A wife takes joy in sharing her husband's troubles. She chose her place at your side, and you chose a place at her side. When secrets creep into a marriage, they push you apart and leave space for lies and distrust."

"I don't lie to her." But hadn't I? I'd kept secrets from her before and Norris was right, it had created distrust between the two of us. I'd worked hard to open myself to her, but here I was still protecting her from myself, even when she begged me not to.

"A secret is a lie to everyone but the one who keeps it,"

Norris advised. "If I may, have you ever considered that you keep these things from her so that you can ignore your own fears? If you share what scares you, you can no longer control the reality of it."

"I don't know how to tell her," I confessed. I didn't know what any of it meant. I had no idea what the repercussions of pursuing my father's past would be.

"Start at the beginning." Norris stood and straightened his jacket. He took a step toward the door but thought better of it. Pausing, he turned to me and placed a hand on my shoulder. "You married a strong woman with a fierce heart. Believe in her as she has believed in you."

Reaching up I clasped his hand in a show of solidarity. Our eyes met and I nodded before releasing my grip. Norris looked to the painting of my father and sighed.

"You should take that down," he suggested.

"It is rather hard to get things done with your father reproaching your every action," I muttered in agreement.

Norris chuckled softly. "It might feel that way, but you should take it down because you must stop seeing yourself through his eyes. Stop looking at yourself from the past and accept the man you have become."

"What kind of man is that?" I whispered, unsure what his answer would be.

"A good one."

CHAPTER ELEVEN

*L*uggage waited inside the bedroom, and I stared at it, wondering if Clara had bothered to pack for me. Despite my recent conversation with Norris, I had waited for the morning. She was due to leave for Balmoral in an hour. If she wouldn't speak to me, I wouldn't ruin her Christmas. It was a cowardly thing to wait until the last moment, but the the very real possibility that I would spend the holidays drinking bourbon won out over bravery. Even through the walls I could hear the flutter of activity in the nursery. I took one deep breath to steel myself and followed the convenient passage that led from this room to my daughter's. Inside Clara and Penny were busy checking for all the last minute items they needed to gather for travel.

I watched my wife, her hair gathered into a knot at the back of her neck and her slender body showcasing a lovely navy dress that offset the fairness of her skin. I imagined

slipping it from her shoulders and kissing each of the
dozens of freckles that dotted them. We'd seen each other
in passing, but I had done my level best to give her the
space she desired. It wasn't a selfless act. It was one of
desperation. I'd hoped time would heal the rift between us,
and that if I could show her that I respected her wishes it
would undo her pain over that night. But she fled from me
in the halls and took her meals in private. She had granted
me access to Elizabeth, but on those occasions, she'd left
me alone with Penny. With each passing day my resolve to
allow her to find her way back to me—if she so chose—
weakened a bit.

Penny glanced up and froze. Of course, it wouldn't go
unnoticed to the nanny that my wife and I weren't speaking. Her sudden awkwardness caught Clara's attention. My
wife swiveled to face me, and we stared across the room at
each other.

"Penny, will you go check in with the driver?" I asked
her. It was a pointless errand, meant to send her away. We
all knew it, but she curtsied and dashed away. I didn't wait
for Clara's reaction. Instead, I went to Elizabeth, who was
busy gnawing on a wooden block on the floor.

"Come to your daddy, Princess." I picked her up and
held her close. Without Clara by my side, our daughter had
been the one tangible link I had to my wife.

Clara had made it clear that she had no intention of
leaving me. Or had I merely imagined that? The thought of
losing either of them was unbearable. I buried my nose
against Elizabeth's fine curls and breathed in her baby

scent. I'd always known that I didn't deserve Clara, but I knew now that I needed her. I wouldn't survive without them. After a few moments, I decided I couldn't avoid it any longer. "Can we talk?"

She planted her hands on her hips as if considering the request. Finally, she shrugged. "We'll have the entire trip to Scotland to talk."

So, she did expect me to come. I hadn't expected that to be the case, so I hadn't made preparations. "I won't be coming," I told her softly. I felt a small squeeze of hope when disappointment flitted over her face. "Not yet, poppet."

Facing her, I knew that I had to find a way to put the past behind me before I could give all of myself to my family. I planned to take Norris's advice. Clara needed to know what I had been keeping from her. But that wouldn't make the issue go away. If I ran away to Scotland, this mystery wouldn't be solved. Once I laid it to rest, I'd be able to be the father and husband they both deserved.

Clara turned away, but I caught the slide of her throat. Was she swallowing back tears? I couldn't stop myself from going to her. With Elizabeth in my arms, I couldn't touch her but I needed to be near her. I needed her to know I was there. When I reached her, she shook her head. "You have to come! Everyone is expecting you, and Elizabeth will be disappointed."

"She won't know." As much as I'd like to think that my daughter missed me in my absence, she was far too young to realize when I was missing. I couldn't blame Clara for pretending to be concerned for our daughter though.

Clara dared a glance at me, tears swimming in her eyes. "She will, and Edward will want you there."

Apparently, she was going to continue to cast her own desires onto others. I couldn't allow her to suffer over this situation any longer. "Sit down."

"Don't order me around," she snapped.

"Please sit down and talk to me." This was what she wanted. She'd begged me to open up to her. Why did she have to be so infuriatingly stubborn and beautiful and kissable? To my relief, she sat down in one of the nursery's rocking chairs. Crossing her arms, she glared at me. I hadn't expected her to make this easy, but how could facing my angry wife be scarier than addressing Parliament?

"I'm listening."

It was a start. I decided it was best to jump right in rather than risk testing her patience. "First of all, I don't want to push you away, and I don't want to keep secrets from you."

"Then stop keeping secrets from me," she said in a flat voice.

"Okay, I'll try that." I paced in front of her, clutching our daughter. Elizabeth seemed to sense my anxiety and she placed a tiny, reassuring hand on my cheek.

Clara held her arms out. I hesitated, not wanting to give up my lifeline. Then I thought better and handed her the baby. I needed Clara to stay calm. I needed her to listen.

There was a better chance of that if her maternal instinct was turned on.

"I've spent most of my life keeping secrets. My secrets. My family's secrets." It was an excuse, but I needed her to understand where I was coming from. "I don't want to keep things from you. I don't think I even mean to most of the time."

Clara raised her eyebrow in doubt. "That might be true, but when I ask you directly, you still refuse to open up. I thought we were past this when we got married…"

"And I keep doing it," I finished before she could. "I wish I had some brilliant insight as to why I'm so thick. I really do. All I can do is try and plead for your mercy when I fail."

"You can start by telling me what has you so worried that you're acting like a git."

This time I raised an eyebrow. "You're sounding more British everyday, poppet."

"God, I hope so. I'm the Queen of England," she shot back. Her eyes followed me as I made another loop around the room. "Will you sit down? You're making me nervous."

"I'm making you nervous." I laughed at the absurdity of that idea. "I've spent the last week going crazy wondering if you still love me."

"It's not a light switch, X. I can't just turn it off." She paused to glare at me before adding, "Even when I wish I could."

I deserved it, but it stung all the same. I never wanted to stop loving Clara. I could no sooner give her up than I could cut out my own heart. I had driven her to this point, and I had to atone for that. I thought of Norris's words of wisdom. I had to start at the beginning and hope that she would hear me through to the end. I cleared by throat and began. "Sometimes I think I keep secrets from you because I don't want to admit that some things are true."

"Do you hear how stupid that sounds?"

Trust my wife to not make this easy on me.

"I've been looking into my father's death." I had told her otherwise, but I'd never believed she was foolish enough to accept that. Judging from her non-reaction to this bit of news, I hadn't managed to convince her. "I told myself I wasn't lying or keeping secrets, but I was."

A smile twitched at her lips. I imagined she was enjoying my admission. I didn't often confess to being wrong. "Continue."

"I felt it was my duty. To him. To our family. I suppose I have a bit of an obsessive personality."

This time the smile broke fully. I could have fallen at her feet. Instead, I took the chair across from hers. "I have a brother."

A weight lifted from me as soon as I said it, but it remained to be seen whether I'd simply handed my burden over to her.

"I've met him," she said suspiciously. It was an understandable reaction. "Are you feeling well?"

"Not Edward," I said quietly, silencing her clever retorts. "My father had another son. He hid it from us."

"Who is he?" She shook her head as if rattling loose

cobwebs. I knew exactly what she was feeling. It was one of the reasons I'd kept it from her in the first place.

"I don't know. I asked Brexton to look into it."

There were a million questions she could ask. Why did my father hide it? What would I do when I found him? Did he want to be found? Did he know about me? They were all the questions I asked myself when I found out. Instead Clara asked the one question that hadn't occurred to me. "Does it matter?"

"Of course, it does."

"Why?" she pressed. Elizabeth began to squirm in her arms and Clara released her to the ground. She crawled off, and I couldn't help but note the vacancy in my wife's arms. I didn't dare try my luck though.

"He could be behind everything."

Clara sighed. It was heavy sound as if she'd been carrying it for a long time. "I know the world hasn't given you a lot of reason to have faith in people. But you have to stop expecting the worst."

"I don't expect the worst." It was a ludicrous idea.

"You wouldn't tell me about this because you didn't think I could handle it. How am I doing?" she asked pointedly.

I didn't want to admit that she had a point. Brex had made a similar observation.

"If," she continued, "you wanted to find him because you were curious or because he's your brother, I could understand that. But you don't have to seek out conspiracies everywhere."

"I nearly lost you to a conspiracy," I reminded her. I would never take that chance again. There was good reason for me to be unsatisfied by the findings of the inquest into my father's murder. It had revealed that whoever helped Daniel was still at-large, and he had no problem sacrificing his puppets to keep his identity unknown. I'd thought it would end with Hammond. His untimely death proved otherwise. "I can't chance it."

"Life is too short to chase sorrow." Clara's eyes pleaded with me. "Be here with us. With me."

"I'm trying to," I promised her.

"Why aren't you coming to Scotland?" she asked in a small voice.

"I need to see this through. Maybe you're right, and it doesn't matter. Maybe I need to look at this from a different perspective, but I know I'm close." She turned away from me, and I tried to see the situation through her eyes. "Clara, I am not choosing this over you."

"It feels like you are."

"I will never choose anything over you." I meant it with every fiber of my being. "I will be with you on Christmas morning."

"What about the night before or the day after?" she demanded. A sob wrenched free and she stood, trying to hide her emotions. Now she was the one keeping something from me. I could see it in her eyes. I had no right to demand she share it with me though. Not after I'd been so stubborn about opening up to her. Dashing over to Elizabeth, she picked her up. "They'll be waiting for us."

I blocked her at the doorway. I didn't dare touch her. Not yet. Not while things were still so tenuous between us. She hadn't forgiven me, and I hadn't apologized. But I leaned forward and kissed Elizabeth's forehead. She cooed appreciatively. "You are always with me."

"Prove it," she commanded me softly. "Come back to me. When you've let this go. Find your peace and then find me."

Without thinking I reached out and brushed her cheek. "I will always find you."

Before she could stop me, I bent and captured her lips. After so long without contact, I expected to be driven by my more primitive needs, but as soon as our mouths met, it was enough. The bittersweet contact, full of longing and hope, tugged the shattered pieces of us back together. When she broke away, she didn't turn from me. Instead she allowed me to press my forehead to hers. We lingered like that for a moment.

"I love you," I whispered, "and I will prove I'm worthy of you."

She didn't respond. I watched her leave, feeling ripped apart. Clara was my soul, and as she walked away, I questioned my decision. She might not understand why I had to see this through, but I did. So long as she was breathing, I would give everything, even my own life, to protect her. It was one sacrifice that I would never question, even if she did.

I'd started at the beginning as Norris had suggested. Now it was time to see this to the end.

CHAPTER TWELVE

Christmas had come early to Scotland, indeed. When Edward claimed the tree didn't meet his standards, he had apparently overcorrected to remedy the problem. Now the Christmas tree took up at least half of the estate's family parlor. The rest of the house was dripping to the core: fresh garlands covered mantels and wrapped around stair railings, large arrangements of poinsettias and roses dotted every flat surface. There were so many presents it looked as if St. Nicholas had come early. Clara stared at them, wondering exactly where she would put the presents she had brought. A familiar arm dropped over her shoulder and she leaned against her brother-in-law.

"Did I do okay?" he asked.

"It's perfect," she promised him. "But I don't know how we're going to fit a wedding in here."

Edward swiveled toward her, his teeth biting into his

lower lip. He looked guilty as if he was about to deliver bad news. It wouldn't be the first time he called off his wedding, but this time might be his last. Clara was getting as tired of the delays as David. Perhaps, they could stage a coup.

"Nope." She clicked her tongue in disapproval. "You aren't getting out of it this time."

"That's not it." He rushed to assure her. "It's just the more David and I talk about it, the more we want only close family at the wedding."

"Do I qualify?" Clara asked.

"Shut up." He ignored the question rather than pander to her sarcasm. It was further proof that he knew her well. "I know your family will be here for Christmas, and while I love the Bishops—"

Clara cut him off with a raised finger. "You don't need to say any more than that. My lips are sealed."

Planning a clandestine wedding turned out to be harder than she thought. Edward filled her in on the numerous preparations the housekeeper, Mrs. Watson, had been busy making. She insisted that there be a cake, but that meant that they had to hide a cake.

"It's not just any cake," Edward told her. "She went up to the village herself and picked up a pair of lovebirds for the top of it. She was terribly disappointed when they told her they didn't have two grooms."

"If only everyone were as bighearted as Mrs. Watson." Clara couldn't help laughing. Edward had spent nearly every family holiday here since he was a baby, which meant the woman had watched him grow up. It was impossible not to love Edward, and his fiancée, David, was quite lovely, too.

"What will we wear?" Clara asked, motioning toward the couch. She wanted to hear all the details. A wedding was exactly what she needed to take her mind off the bombshell that Alexander had dropped before she left.

Just thinking about it made her twitch. If Alexander had told her, had he told Edward? It didn't seem a good idea to bring it up when he was preoccupied with his wedding but he deserved to know. She pushed the thought out of her mind. It could wait. Everything could wait. Right now, the only thing that mattered was that one of the people she loved most dearly was about to say *I do*.

"I wanted to wear white," Edward said dryly, "but David insists that no one will buy it."

"What about a veil?" Clara teased.

"He said we could go in drag for our second wedding," Edward reassured her. Lounging back into the well-worn leather sofa, he crossed his arms behind his head. "David insisted we pack our tuxedos for New Year's Eve."

"That was forward thinking of him," Clara pointed out.

"Exactly." Edward nodded as if this had not escaped his attention either. "In truth, you can't tell that man he has to miss out on an opportunity to dress up, even if it's only a party of six."

"Six?" she repeated. He had really meant it when he said he wanted to keep it in the family.

"Well, I suppose Elizabeth counts as seven." Edward

counted out loud on his fingers. "And then there's Mrs. Watson, so that's eight with you and Alexander, and Smith and Belle."

Clara forced a smile onto her lips, hoping he couldn't see the hint of the pain hearing her husband's name caused her. Thankfully, Edward was too wrapped up in the promise of marital bliss to notice.

Alexander had promised he'd find a way to her. She hadn't wanted to be the one to tell him that Edward was finally going to tie the knot. If Alexander had promised to be there on Christmas, she would plan on it. It would devastate her if he didn't show, but she would step in before she allowed him to miss his brother's wedding. But she wouldn't call him until the absolute last minute. Part of her wanted him to feel as alone as he'd made her feel. Another part of her felt ashamed for that thought. Alexander had opened up to her, and when he had revealed the truth – that he had a brother neither of them knew about — she'd understood some of his hesitance to share. But this was about more than keeping one secret. It was about what was important to her. If their marriage was going to say strong, he needed to learn to compromise, especially when it came to what he chose to share with her.

"Earth to Clara," Edward called, waving his hand in the air until he got her attention. "You're sitting next to me but it seems like you're miles away."

"I just realized that I didn't get you a wedding present," she lied. This was why she couldn't continue to put up with Alexander's secrets. It meant constantly forcing her to keep secrets from the rest of the people in her life. Where did it end?

With her, she decided, and that was final.

"Don't worry about it." Edward dismissed her concern. "It's not as if we need anything, and I didn't exactly give you time to shop."

"You'll have to settle for the pleasure my company," she told him.

He dazzled her with a boyish grin. In that moment, the difference between him and his brother was clear. It was easy to see their age difference or Edward's curly hair compared to Alexander's black locks, but it was the quickness of his smile that set him apart from his older brother. Edward pushed up his horn rim spectacles. "That's all I ever want."

"Ever?" Belle cried out in mock sadness, interrupting the duo. Edward shot off the couch and ran to hug her. Clara felt a slight pang of jealousy in her chest as she watched the two of them. She had been the one to introduce them, and while she counted them both as her best friends, there was a little part of her that felt left out when she saw them together. Although she had to admit she had given them plenty of crises to bond over through the last couple of years. She shook the irrational reaction away. Between the Christmas season and her fight with Alexander, she was being silly. When the two broke apart, Belle grabbed Edward's hands. "Tell me about the wedding."

He cast a mischievous glance over at Clara. "That seems to be everyone's favorite topic."

They spent the afternoon plotting and planning. They also took turns picking Elizabeth up off the floor after numerous tumbles.

"You've yet to get your sea legs," Edward told his niece, hugging her closely.

"Don't encourage her," Clara warned. "Once she really starts walking it's all over. We'll have to baby-proof everything, and I'll never be able to catch up with her."

"Don't you have a nanny?" He asked her pointedly, looking around the room as if one might suddenly appear. Apparently, Edward presumed the royal family had their very own Mary Poppins.

"We do," Clara said, "but I want to do most of it. I'm her mother, after all."

"She's making up for her own mother," Belle interjected, casting a knowing glance at Edward.

"I think it's nice," Edward said. "I wish I had known my mother."

The girls paused awkwardly and looked to one another.

"Don't be like that," Edward commanded. "You two aren't the only ones who get to be sentimental this time of year."

"Anything is better than my mother," Belle said.

"Mine?" Clara teased.

"I will trade Madeline Bishop for Mary Stuart any day of the week," Belle promised her.

"How is your mother?" Edward asked.

Over the last year, Belle's relationship with her mother had gone from tense to unbearable almost overnight. That largely had to do with Belle's decision to sell her interest in the family estate. The move left Mary without a home. It was merely a technicality, though. Belle had sold her interest to her half-brother, and despite the way his step-mother had treated him over the years, John Stuart had displayed an incredible benevolence by allowing Mary to stay in his home.

"She's spending Christmas with John," Belle informs them.

"Is that safe?" Clara asked. Having known Bill for years, she was well aware of the danger Mary Stuart posed to anyone in isolation.

"She mentioned going to the neighbor's for Christmas morning." Belle shrugged. Whatever suited her mother was fine by her. "He's some politician, and my mother just loves him."

"And you don't?" Edward said.

Belle shook her head furiously. "There's something about him."

"Yes, the fact that he likes your mother," Clara said.

"That might be it," Belle admitted with a laugh.

Mrs. Watson bustled into the room, a flurry of skirts and aprons. She held out a slip of paper for inspection.

"I need one of you to review this, and I don't care which," she said in a thick Scottish brogue. Clara knew the woman less well than most of the others, and she was eager to impress her. Watson was one of the Cambridge men's maternal influences during their youth. Clara dutifully took the sheet and skimmed it.

"I know everyone is busy planning the wedding," Watson continued in a tizzy, "but I need to worry about Christmas supper. There will be far more people here for that."

There would, indeed. This year, the three of them had hatched a plan to revise the typical Balmoral family Christmas. While it had been tradition in Albert's time to extend an invitation to nearly all the branches of the family, Clara had expressed her desire to leave the royal brat pack out of her holiday festivities. Edward had wholeheartedly agreed. Alexander's and Edward's cousins weren't always on their best behavior, and they had never been anything but rude to Clara. Coupling that with the fact that Edward had stayed in the closet longer due to his fear of what they might do, it had been unanimously agreed that they would make their own family this year. It wouldn't be all smooth sailing, though.

After much discussion, it had been decided that all of the Bishops should be invited. Lola was well-loved by Belle and Edward, but David still felt a little annoyance over her misunderstanding with Edward. It had led to an unwanted kiss between the two. Still, she could be counted on to be on her best behavior. Madeline and Harold Bishop were another story. Clara's parents had been in couples counseling for the better part of the last year, and as far as she knew, her father had finally ended his affair with his younger business partner. She hadn't bothered to ask him herself, though. Undoubtedly, there would be tension.

Smith had no living family, and Belle was more than

happy to leave her mother off the invite list. The only person representing the newly formed Stewart-Price clan would be Aunt Jane, who had an uncanny knack for knowing when to step in and went to stay out. Clara almost asked Edward if he considered asking her to stay for the wedding, but she wanted to respect his wishes. If it had been up to her when she was planning her own wedding, it probably would have only been close friends, too. As it turned out, she'd gotten just that, but not because she wanted it. Her actual wedding vows had been said in a hospital room. She was determined that Edward's fairytale would be more romantic.

Edward peeked over Clara's shoulder. "This all looks grand to me." He stood and locked his arm to hers. "Now, if we could discuss the filling of the cake."

The old housekeeper might need to worry about Christmas dinner, but everyone else's minds were on the wedding.

CHAPTER THIRTEEN

*I*t had come to this. He had opened his door to a wolf. Georgia looked out of place standing in his foyer. Then again in her leather pants and motorcycle jacket, she looked out of place most everywhere. She certainly didn't belong there. This was his present and his future. She was firmly in his past. She turned in a circle then shoved her hands into her leather jacket and whistled, "You really are a changed man, Price."

"Yes, I am," he assured her.

But just having her here suggested the contrary. This was the second time he had seen her in a month.

He'd taken a few days to consider the information she had given him and to see Belle safely off to Scotland. Knowing who was behind Hammond and the conspiracy that had nearly claimed his wife's life didn't mean he knew what to do about it. There had been a time when Smith Price wouldn't have thought twice.

GENEVA LEE

He would have acted on instinct. But, his instincts hadn't always proven wise. Instead, he had digested this news slowly and taken time to consider all of his options.

"I've been thinking about what you told me," he said to Georgia.

She held up a hand. "I have a feeling I need a drink for this. Or are you going to pretend to be sober again?"

His eyes narrowed, but he tipped his head toward the sitting room. Once they reached it, he pointed to the bar cart.

"Not joining me?" she asked.

If someone had told Smith that Georgia was the original serpent in the Garden of Eden, he would have believed it. How many times would he fall victim to her dangling forbidden fruit in front of him? He shook his head. What was the point of any of this if he didn't learn from his mistakes?

"Suit yourself," she shrugged as she uncapped a crystal decanter and poured herself a bourbon. She didn't bother to sit. Instead, she leaned against the wall, sipping slowly. She was here on business and they both knew that. "So, what do you want to know?"

"Has anything changed?" he asked. He doubted it, but it seemed a prudent place to start.

"Not really," she hedged. He sensed she was holding something back. Of course, she would. That was how she operated.

"Has your team found anything new?" he pressed.

128

"No," she said finally, "because I told them to stop looking."

Smith prided himself on his ability to bluff, but she'd caught him off guard. Surprise passed over his face before he could stop it. She had been so sure that Oliver Jacobson was the one behind the attacks. Had something changed? He cleared his throat. "Why?"

"You asked me the other day if it would be the Crown's justice or my own," she reminded him, and he nodded. "I don't think justice belongs to either of us."

"Who does it belong to?" he asked in a measured voice. This was why it was difficult to accept that Georgia was working for the Crown. She didn't play by their rules. She didn't play by anyone's rules but her own, and it was impossible for an outsider to understand the twisted logic she employed to guide her moral compass.

"It's yours," she told him with a note of finality.

"Mine?" he repeated.

Her lips thinned into a line and she gave him a scathing look of disapproval.

"I don't see how it's my justice," he continued before she cut him off.

"Why am I here, Smith? You called me this time, but I doubt it was for an update."

"I don't know," he said, but it was a bald-faced lie. She'd known him long enough to see right through him, but even if she'd been a complete stranger, his answer was as transparent as glass.

"You want to claim justice as your own," she answered

for him when he could not. "No one could blame you for that. I couldn't blame you for that, because it isn't just about justice. It's about protecting her. You have to know that she's still in danger. You have to see that the clock is ticking on your reprieve. He knows her. He chose her. So long as he breaths, Belle will be a target to him."

"You don't know that," Smith growled. But he did. He had already reached the same conclusion. It was what had driven him to this low point. He'd needed Georgia's help to ensure his wife's safety. Now that he knew the truth, he also knew there were far too many variables for him to turn a blind eye. His stomach twisted under the pressure.

"What's stopping you?" she pressured him.

"The night that Hammond died," he looked up to her, "I went to kill him myself."

"I suspected as much," she confirmed.

So, she believed in his innocence. That meant something to him. Even those closest to him, even the people he trusted, had questioned it when he claimed his innocence. They'd let it go because if it had been Smith that had killed Hammond, no one could blame him.

Georgia knew better than anyone the reasons he had to end that man's life. She might have had even more herself, but she'd been strapped to a hospital bed, fighting for her life.

"I realized I had a choice," his voice was low as he spoke. But it no longer felt that way. Every time he took a fork in the road, it seemed to lead back to the other path. Was this

his destiny all along? To be a killer? How had he ever been stupid enough to believe he could escape it?

"Hammond told me I was free. He acted as if he was giving me the option, but I knew in that moment it was my choice. It has always been my choice. I walked away. I didn't want to be him."

"And now?" she said softly, a tone that contradicted her usual demeanor. This was personal to her as well, and she could no longer pretend that it wasn't. Hammond had twisted both of their lives to suit his purposes. He had been responsible for the death of Smith's father and subsequently the slow death that claimed Smith's mother.

But Georgia had been another story. Hammond had groomed her. He had taught her about pain and he had taught her to want it. Smith couldn't imagine what it would take to break a woman like Georgia Kincaid. He didn't want to. It was enough to make him sick. The first time Hammond had ever put a whip in Smith's hands, introduced him to the seedy underbelly of London's bondage scene, he had also given him Georgia to dominate. It was a dynamic that neither of them appreciated or wanted. But, there had been little choice. Maybe that's why it felt like they were still in this together now, because it had been the two of them since the beginning.

"You still have a choice," Georgia told him. "I'm giving it to you now."

"What do you know about him?" Smith asked. He forced the part of himself that felt disgusted for taking part in this man's inevitable death deep inside himself. This was about Belle. His whole life was her now and he couldn't rest until he had ensured her safety.

"He's married," Georgia informed him. "Two kids that they shipped off to boarding school as soon as they were done teething. Everyone we've spoken to suggests his rise to power in Parliament is only just starting. He keeps his anti-Royal sentiments to a minimum, but our sources believe he's swaying more and more members to his side."

"Why doesn't Alexander just go about it like that?" Smith could curse the man despite his own connections with the royal family. Smith himself wasn't particularly fond of the royalty concept. It helped knowing that Alexander didn't exactly love to be King. Smith might not collect Royal memorabilia, but he didn't wish them harm. "And if Jacobson wants to dismantle the Royal Family, why wouldn't he just proceed through legal avenues?"

"I wish I knew," she told him.

"What else?" Smith prompted. What she'd said so far wasn't enough to go on. He needed information, needed facts. Where did Jacobson live when he was in town? Where was he now? Was he a paranoid man? Smith couldn't help but curse himself for not realizing the monster was within his grasp the day they had gone hunting. It would have been so easy, but harder to cover up. A planned attack meant he stood a chance of getting away with the murder. It was unlikely, but the odds were a little better than shooting a man in cold blood.

"Why don't you want to do it?" Smith asked.

Georgia paused as if considering this. Then she poured

herself another bourbon. "I suppose in a way, Jacobson did me a favor," she admitted. "I would never have been free from Hammond, not until he was dead. That's why I didn't go after Jacobson myself."

"He was the one who ordered the hit on you," Smith pointed out.

At the time, he thought Hammond had been the one behind the attempt on Georgia's life, but the more he considered it, he couldn't bring himself to believe it. Hammond was obsessed with Georgia. He considered her his adoptive daughter, never mind that he'd been bedding her since she was a teenager. It was a perverse relationship to be sure, but one that Smith knew Hammond held dear. It had to have been Jacobson who ordered her death. It was the only thing that made sense.

"Jacobson tried to have me killed." Georgia shrugged, as if this revelation had rolled off her back like a light rain. "There are worse things than death, believe me." It was the closest she had ever come to opening up to Smith about the past she kept hidden. He didn't blame her for wanting Hammond dead. She'd played her part well, pretending to be the dutiful daughter. She'd accepted her role, and at times she had enjoyed it.

That was the difference in Smith's eyes. Whereas his wife had a natural submissive streak that turned on his dominant side, Georgia craved the pain for much less healthy reasons. She treated her body as a sacrifice, and Smith had always seen the reality behind the submission.

133

The shame, and the guilt had driven her to moments far more depraved than even he could imagine.

"Don't look so heartbroken for me," she said, calling him from his thoughts. "I'm no damsel in distress, remember?"

If only that was true, Smith thought. The best thing that could ever happen to Georgia would be if she allowed someone to save her. He couldn't imagine what kind of man that would take. He had an inkling that she couldn't either. Maybe that's why she continued to seek him out. The trouble with Georgia was that she looked in all the wrong places.

"I want specifics," Smith said, deciding to get back to business. He would never be the one to heal Georgia, no matter the sentimental attachment he held for the woman. He hoped she would find someone who could. If she wouldn't act in regards to Jacobson, he would. There was no other choice. He could see that now. All roads led back to the same decision: to stay under the thumb of an evil man or to destroy the danger once and for all. He'd made his choice long ago, and now it was time for the reckoning.

CHAPTER FOURTEEN

"*I* am exhausted," Clara announced, flopping onto the couch beside Edward.

Belle sighed heavily. There went her plans. At some point, she felt it was necessary to take Edward on a stag night. There were plenty of pubs in the nearby village, and even Norris wouldn't be able to argue with letting Clara go for such a reason. The trouble was that poor Clara was always tired.

"Why did you leave the nanny at home again?" Belle asked her.

Clara frowned, as if it was obvious. "She has a family, too. There was no need for her to give up her holidays to take care of my child."

When Clara put it like that, Belle couldn't argue with her selflessness. Still, it presented a problem.

"Why so gloomy?" Edward bumped her shoulder.

"I planned to take her to the pub tonight," Belle

confessed. "I feel like I should give your bachelorhood a proper send-off as your matron of honor."

"I thought I was the matron of honor," Clara pouted.

"You're both the matrons of honor." Edward stepped in before the two got bent out of shape.

"Regardless," Belle said meaningfully, "I wanted to take you on a stag night. It'll be harder when everyone's here for Christmas."

She respected Edward's desire to keep the whole affair a secret, but that did make it a little more difficult. The extended family didn't plan to depart until right before New Year's Eve. That left no time for a night on the town.

"Go on without me," Clara encouraged.

"We couldn't," Belle said, which earned her an eye roll from her best friend.

"You could," Clara corrected her. "And you will. You two are still young and childless. Enjoy it now." She winked at Belle behind Edward's back.

That hadn't occurred to Belle. Not only were Edward's days as a bachelor numbered, if Smith's and her new hobby panned out, hers might be as well. It was hard enough for her to get away from her husband for the evening. How much more difficult would it be when she had a baby's needs to meet as well?

"I feel like I'm missing out on something," Edward said, looking between the two of them.

Belle plastered a smile on her face and shook her head. "I was just thinking of where I would take you first."

"Norris better drive you," Clara interjected.

"Are you saying we can't handle our liquor?" Edward said in mock horror, grabbing his chest as though she had wounded him.

"Nope," Clara retorted. "I'm saying you can't stay out of trouble."

THE ROAD'S END TAVERN sat delightfully at the road's end. It wasn't uncommon for locals to spot the royal family here during the holiday season, so no one batted an eye when Belle and Edward stepped through the battered door. They grabbed a table in the corner and ordered a few pints.

"I wanted to take you to a strip club," Belle told him apologetically. "But my options were limited."

"I think there's a fair chance that if you get any of these men drunk enough, they'll take off their clothes." Edward teased. The two of them looked around the room and then back at each other.

"Maybe we should skip that," Belle suggested.

"So, I've never done a stag night before," Belle told him as their beers arrived.

"I think we're supposed to chase women and howl at the moon," Edward informed her. "I'm afraid I'm not a fount of information on it, either."

She laughed at the image. If the two of them were going to chase a woman, it would be to advise her to wear a different type of shoe with her dress.

"Nevermind a bachelor party. What about a hen night?" Edward suggested. "Is that more suitable?"

Belle shrugged. "I don't know. I never really had one."

"We're terrible at this friend thing, aren't we?" Edward pointed out.

"Maybe." She agreed.

"How about we get pissed and you tell me about the dangers of marriage?" He suggested.

"As long as your spouse doesn't have a murderous employer, I think you'll be all right."

She took a long sip of her beer and pondered what he'd said. Were there things she'd wished she had known before she married Smith? She hadn't had time to really consider her decision. They'd eloped on an impulse, and miraculously, it had worked out. Belle supposed that when you have people trying to murder you, you don't sweat the small stuff.

"You've grown dangerously silent," Edward said, lifting his glass and tapping it to hers. "Care to share?"

"I was trying to think of something to warn you about," she said, "But I can't come up with anything."

Edward groaned, and laid his head on the table. After a moment, he lifted it and gave her a crooked grin. "If only every relationship could be as perfect as yours."

"Mine's not perfect," she reassured him, screwing up her face as if the thought was unpleasant. If he knew the half of it, he would never suggest it.

"You never fight, always have a post-orgasmic glow. Your husband is gorgeous and rich. What don't you have?" It was a rhetorical question, but Belle answered before she could think about it. "A baby."

Edward set his beer glass down. "Is that something we want?"

Belle bit her lip and nodded. She had already come clean to Clara. It was time to open up to Edward as well.

"I suppose my days are numbered," he said sadly.

"What days?" She asked. They would still spend time together. They'd even go out to the bars every once in a while. It took her a second to realize that for the second time this evening, she was treating motherhood as an inevitability instead of an outside possibility. She wanted to slow down, and not get attached to the idea, but it appeared it was too late.

"David will want to adopt," he said, "and then we'll be having play dates instead of pub dates."

Belle scrunched up her nose. "When I think about spending the afternoon with Elizabeth, that doesn't sound so bad." None of them had complained about taking care of Elizabeth because they all adored her. The thought that Belle and Edward could add to the adorable brood didn't scare her.

"At least you can get pregnant," he said casually. "We'll have to adopt."

"You won't have any trouble." She said with a tight smile. "You have the pedigree."

"I suppose I could just walk in and take any baby I like." He said flatly.

"You are the Prince of England," she pointed out.

"I don't think it works that way, but if you're telling me that this whole time I could have been walking in places

GENEVA LEE

and taking whatever I wanted, I feel this should have been brought up sooner."

"It will work out," she reassured him. "It will probably be easier."

"Than your getting pregnant?" Edward asked. "I doubt it."

"I've seen both you and Smith. Somewhere, the two of you are at the height of a Darwinian evolution chart. He could probably impregnate you just by looking at you."

Belle's eyes found her glass, and she stared at the tiny bubbles floating to the top of the golden liquid.

"I hope it's that easy," she said in a small voice.

Edward reached over and took her hand. "It will be." He had no reason to believe otherwise.

Belle hadn't shared her miscarriage with him, or her fears about getting pregnant. Maybe if he knew, he wouldn't have said it, but something about the reassurance, the confidence in his voice, made her believe it too. She squeezed his hand, then lifted her glass.

"I'm not pregnant yet. Let's drink."

CHAPTER FIFTEEN

It felt good to leave the house, although if I were being honest this was like a second home to me. The seat vibrated as the engines roared to life. In another life I'd belonged here. It was strange how easily pieces of who I was had slipped away over the last two years. Nearly all of them had been filled by her, and I would have given up far more of myself if it had been necessary. But while Clara brought out the fighter in me, this was one part of myself that I needed to reclaim. I had been a pilot once, a soldier, a leader in more than name and title, and I had saved men's lives because of it. Clara was still breathing today because of my time on the battlefront.

Brexton's voice filled my earpiece, and I turned to look at my friend.

"I don't think I'm supposed to let you fly, Poor Boy."

"Try to stop me," I said into my mic.

Other people were out doing their Christmas shopping,

but nostalgia appealed to me on a very different level. I flipped a few switches and signaled to Brex that we were ready. Then we were airborne. I hadn't flown since that fateful night that nearly claimed Clara's life. Not really. I'd been on private planes and commercial jets. I'd done my fair share of traveling, but that was flying as a passenger, and it was a hell of a lot different than being a pilot.

Brex had put up a minimal fight about letting me take one of the helicopters. Although he had transitioned to my security team, he was still an acting officer of the Royal Air Force. That had certain perks. Whereas my own requests were met with deaf ears and red tape, Brex had gotten a hold of a chopper immediately.

"When I said we needed to talk in private," Brex called over our comms, "this isn't what I meant."

I didn't have to look at him to know he was grinning from ear to ear.

This is how we had met. We had formed a lifelong bond based on our time in the field. I liked to brag that Brex had kept me alive during that time, and he had. All the men I'd flown had kept me alive. I had been in a dark place then, and while I never cared if I came back, I wasn't going to lose any of them. They'd saved me simply by being there. I got the impression that Brex had entirely different reasons for becoming a pilot. Most of them could be found under short skirts.

I couldn't blame him. I'd be lying if I said I'd never used my uniform to catch a woman's attention. Of course, I'd had certain other advantages in that area.

We made our way over London, flying low enough to take in Big Ben and Parliament. It was my turn to grin boyishly as we flew over the London Eye. The romantic in me decided to come out to play when I spotted the place where I had proposed to Clara.

"So," I asked through my mic, "how long have you been seeing Georgia?"

"Every day. We work together," Brex retorted.

"That's not what I meant, brother."

With the heart of London behind us, we headed toward the countryside. I needed to get away and be somewhere where I wasn't surrounded by the constant pressures of my title.

"We're not seeing each other," Brex said after a moment. "You know her pretty well. What's her story?"

I didn't know where to begin with that one. My history with Georgia wasn't up for discussion, but I didn't want to leave Brex out in the cold. There were things he needed to know about her if he wanted to pursue her. Like so many other men, he might have fallen for her attitude and looks without glimpsing what lay beneath. I had to tread carefully. The intimate details of what had happened between Georgia and I in my younger years wasn't something I liked to share, and Georgia prided herself on being discreet. She wouldn't appreciate Brexton finding out that way, either. I did, however, have an out.

"I've known her a long time," I admitted as the wind picked up around us. It was rainy in the countryside today, and it blew in misty sheets against the glass. "I didn't catch up with her until recently, though. She worked for Hammond."

"I know that," Brex said.

Of course he would've been privy to her files, but how deeply had he read up on her?

"What do you know about her, Brex?" I asked him. There was no need to be coy if he already had insight in Georgia's past.

"I know she turned on Hammond. But there's something about her. I didn't want to invade her privacy."

It was a strangely touching gesture for a man who spent most of his time invading knickers. "She owned a club," I told him, "one of Hammond's holdings. It was a BDSM club." Surely he could fill in the blanks from that.

"You mean like whips and shit?" Brexton asked.

I couldn't decide if it was curiosity or apprehension in his voice.

"And shit," I confirmed. "Really rough shit."

"Damn." Brexton let out a low whistle. "So you think she likes that kind of stuff?"

"Yes, I do," I told him. That was as firm as I would be on the matter. He didn't need any more confirmation from me about what Georgia Kinkade was into.

There was a long, awkward silence.

"What is it?" I asked him.

"So do you think if I said I was into that stuff she'd go out on a date with me?"

If I wasn't in the middle flying an aircraft that weighed

several tons, I would've found something to smash my head against.

"I don't think you really date in that scenario." How much more information could I give him without indoctrinating him to the entire world of bondage?

"I don't know."

"Google it."

"I'll take it under advisement."

Despite the wind I could hear the sarcasm in his voice. "There's a good spot."

We put down in a field. It was empty save for a few sheep, but when we got out, rolling green hills smelled of manure.

"Ah, the countryside," I said in a flat voice.

"You were the one who wanted to go for a ride." Brex took off his helmet and tossed it into his seat, and I followed suit.

In case he hadn't realized, I was pretty serious about this whole confidentiality thing. When Brex had informed me he had finally tracked down his special assignment, I decided then and there that I would go to whatever lengths necessary to ensure there would be no leaks.

"So you found him," I said, pulling off my gloves.

"I found his mother," Brex informed me. "From the looks of it, that'll have to do."

"He lives with his mum?" I tried hard not to be judgmental, but what kind of a guy was this?

"He seems to be some kind of nomad. He has a couple apartments here or there."

"He has more than one?" This was a surprise, and more than a little disconcerting. I had my suspicions regarding this secret brother of mine. Finding out that he kept houses in more than one place did nothing to allay them.

"He's into some sort of racing," Brex explained. "His mom lives in Silverstone."

"I wonder how he got into racing," I said sarcastically. The little village sat right outside Silverstone Circuit, one of the world's premier race tracks. "Is he any good?"

"I told you he has a couple apartments." Brex grinned. "He can't be that bad."

"Is there any indication that..." I trailed away. Brex didn't share my suspicions regarding my father's secret family, but I think he understood why I had them.

"None, as far as I can tell. They're good, upstanding citizens. The mother's a war widow, and other than his penchant for dangerous driving he hasn't gotten into any trouble."

"But he's gotten into trouble for driving?" I asked.

"He's had a few tickets. And some crashes," Brex added on as an afterthought.

Given his occupation, this wasn't a surprise. I breathed deeply, enjoying the remnants of rain in the air.

"How can you do that, man?" Brex asked, pinching his nose with his fingers. "It smells like shit out here."

"In the city we have smog," I reminded him. Besides, the two of us had smelled much worse things in the time we'd known each other. "So who are they?"

"Her name is Rachel Stone, and we can find nothing on

her. And I do mean nothing."

"Nothing?" I repeated. That was impossible. "Did you tell them why we were looking into her?"

"I kept that to myself." Brex shot me an incredulous look, like I'd wounded his pride. "But yeah, no intelligence. No background. It's almost like she never existed."

"My father," I said, and Brex didn't question me. An ordinary woman didn't just *not* exist. She had been covered up, but evidently not well enough.

"He's a little easier to get information on, considering his high-profile occupation."

So he really was a racer. I'd have to look into him further.

"Her name is Rachel Stone," Brex told me. "She's 48 years old, and that's all we know about her. We found a few pictures, but there's no employment history, nothing. She draws a small pension from the armed forces in the name of her husband."

"And a monthly salary from my father," I added with annoyance. Dad had gone to a lot of trouble to make certain no one found her. Why? What had she had on him to guarantee his silence and cooperation?

"I want to meet her," I said after a while.

"That is not a good idea," Brex advised.

I tilted my head back to the helicopter. "And that was?"

"Am I going to talk you out of this?" Brex asked.

"You can try, but it's a waste of breath."

"Can I at least escort you?"

"Send me her files."

"And then we'll talk about this further, right?" Brex prompted.

"And her address," I added. "Tomorrow I'm going to Silverstone."

148

The village of Silverstone had none of the flash of the nearby racing track for which it was known. I couldn't help but chuckle as I passed a sign that read *please drive safely*. It was a well-meant warning that no doubt fell on deaf ears. The area was known for the racing track, and I suspected they had their fair share of local teens angling to become part of the action. The tiny town consisted mostly of 19th-century brick and stone houses. Every few meters sat a tiny pub where the locals went for an evening draught.

Turning the Range Rover onto a slender strip of pavement that barely passed as a road, I found the address I was looking for. I pulled over a few houses down and considered my options. I came all the way here, so it made sense to see this through. But now that the answers I'd sought were within my grasp, I wanted to turn around. A few older gentlemen wearing driving caps and tweed jackets ambled past and nodded their heads. If they recognized me it didn't show. I couldn't expect such luck for long.

"This is what you wanted," I told myself. Had it really come to this? Coaching myself through a confrontation with my father's past while sitting on the side of the road in the middle of nowhere? In that moment, it didn't matter that I was the king of England. It didn't matter that I had faced war and assassins. What did matter was why I was here. I came to find the truth, and I wouldn't find it sitting in a car.

Last night, I had read the file on Rachel Stone. It had been alarmingly brief. There wasn't much to say about this woman who'd commanded so much of my father's attention—or at least his money. She was a widow, and she moved to Silverstone shortly before her son's birth. There were no criminal records or scandalous news articles. If my father had paid for her discretion, she performed that task admirably. There was even less about Anderson Stone. I had ordered Brexton to supply me with information as it came in. That meant we had a lot to learn about the Stone family. It was wise he didn't want me to come. I should have listened to him, but I had never been very good at listening to anyone.

That character flaw left me to wonder if my father had tried to tell me about his other son. I had laid awake in bed, searching my memories for some clue. But if he had left any—other than the mysterious bank account—I had been too dense to see it.

As I sat there, a young man walked by with a Christmas tree braced over his shoulder. I froze, hoping to catch a glimpse of his face. Presumably, Anderson Stone would want to spend the holidays with his mother. I had seen photos of him, mostly on his Facebook account, but I wasn't certain what he'd look like in person. When the man turned, I was relieved and disappointed to see it wasn't him. However, the Christmas tree had been a reminder that I had my own family to think of. I had promised Clara I would see this to the end and then I would find her. The thought of my wife was the catalyst I needed to open the Range Rover's door.

Gravel crunched underfoot as I walked a few paces back to the house. It was an unassuming brick box, a plume of smoke curled from the chimney and a single string of Christmas lights decorated the front door. I paused my hand on the antique knocker and then struck it. Inside a woman's voice called out merrily, "I'll be right there, love."

A few moments later the door opened to reveal an older woman, her sandy blonde hair streaked with gray and her blue eyes shining brightly. She blinked a few times as if she had opened the door to a ghost. Then her mouth fell open. She closed it quickly and stepped to the side. "Won't you come in?"

Her recovery was admirable. Then again, I supposed she had expected this day to come. When I began looking into my father's personal life, I knew I would uncover secrets. She must have known that I would as well. I hesitated on the threshold. I was the one who had questioned her motives and her allegiance. If she was the threat I suspected, I was walking into a viper's nest.

"I won't bite," she assured me. Despite the tension of the situation, she was smiling. I stepped inside, and she closed the door behind me. "I never imagined finding Albert's son on my doorstep."

I raised an eyebrow. If my information was true, she'd had Albert's son under her roof. I kept the jibe to myself.

The house was, for lack of a better term, homey. It still retained much of its historical charm with slightly crooked walls and creaking floorboards. There wasn't much to it, but then again, I lived in a palace. She let me through a quaint hallway into a cheery kitchen with butter yellow walls and checked curtains hanging on the windows.

"Would you like some tea?" She didn't wait for my reply. Instead she began to fill the tea kettle before placing it on the hob. "I'm afraid I don't have any fancy tea to brew. I expect you're used to something a mite better than what I get in town."

"I'm not picky," I said with a shrug. Nothing about this situation was going according to plan. Not that I had a plan. I hated to admit it, I had anticipated more drama.

"You must have questions for me." She took a seat at the small kitchen table and gestured for me to join her. I sat opposite her and searched for what to say.

"You are Rachel Stone?" Now seemed like a good time to clarify that fact, before I started spilling the family secrets.

She nodded. "And you are Alexander. I suppose you don't remember me."

There were a lot of things I expected her to say, but that had not been one of them. Should I remember her? She had obviously played an important role in my father's life, but I had no recollection of her being part of mine. "I thought we hadn't met."

"Not since you were a boy." She shook her head as if recalling some memory that had grown dusty with age. "I worked at the palace."

The high-pitched whistle of the tea kettle interrupted her recollection. She jumped up to take it off the flame, leaving me a moment to collect myself after this revelation. She had worked at the palace? That had not been in her file. Had my father covered it up? Why had he gone to such lengths to protect her? Before I could theorize, she returned with two mugs and a selection of teabags.

I cleared my throat, and asked the first thing that came into mind, "what did you do there?"

"I was household staff. I brought tea and biscuits and the newspaper." She dipped a teabag into water and continued, "It wasn't an exciting job, but most of my family had worked in public service. My late husband included."

I seized my opportunity. Any reluctance I had felt asking about her personal life vanished when she brought it up herself. "I suppose you know why I'm here."

"You want to know about your brother," she guessed, laying to rest any possibility that there had been a mistake.

I did have another brother. Even after being told weeks ago, it was difficult to wrap my mind around. The idea that my own flesh and blood had been walking around for the last 25 years without my knowledge seemed impossible.

"Amongst other things. I want to know why he was kept a secret, and how you met my father, and—"

She cut me off. "Maybe I should start at the beginning."

That seemed like a pretty good idea, so I nodded.

"As I mentioned, I worked on the Royal household staff. Initially, I did laundry and worked in the kitchen. After your mother died, I took over some of the domestic duties she had preferred to handle." Rachel gave me a small encouraging smile as if she knew how I was feeling. "I never took over for your mother, Alexander. But someone had to bring the tea. That's how it started.

"I had just lost my husband, and I needed to keep myself busy. One day your father had been drinking, and I came into his study. He asked me to sit down. I had no idea what to expect. Your father was a private man, and most of the staff considered him aloof at best."

"And snooty at worst?" I offered. This earned me a laugh.

"Yes," she agreed. "I knew a very different Albert. He only wanted to talk. I think he was lonely, which is something I understood. From then on, I took his tea to him every day. At first, we talked about the weather or soccer matches. Trivial things. Slowly, he began to open up to me about losing Elizabeth. I listened, and then one day, I

154

opened up to him about losing Todd. It was less a romance than a friendship."

"I have a half-brother that suggests otherwise," I said dryly.

"You are very like him," she said, not noticing how I cringed at the suggestion. "We comforted one another. I doubt that we were the first adults to find solace in bed. If it had been a romance, it would have been doomed. When we slept together, we were imagining other people."

"And then you got pregnant?" If she was going to accuse me of being like my father, then I would be blunt. I couldn't quite see the picture she was painting, although I knew a thing or two about seeking refuge in sex.

She sighed as if giving up on her trip down memory lane. Rachel squared her shoulders and leveled her gaze at me. "I did. It was unplanned, but not entirely unwanted. My husband and I had planned to have a family when he returned from the Gulf. That never happened. Instead, your father gave me a child and a chance to have the family I thought I had lost forever."

"Does he..." I trailed away. It was the one question I wanted to ask. The question I had come here to ask. Now, somehow, I wasn't certain I wanted to know. Gathering my courage, I forced myself to ask. "Does he know who his father is?"

"As far as Anders is concerned, his father died on the front," she said pointedly.

No man could be that stupid. I didn't say this out loud.

Instead, I shifted uncomfortably in my chair. The math didn't add up. If her husband had died in the Gulf and my mother died the same year, that meant she was either lying about her relationship with my father or she was lying to her son.

"Let me guess," she said, interrupting my thoughts, "the timeline doesn't add up. Of course, Anders knows that Todd Stone can't be his father. I suppose everyone does. It doesn't take a genius to look at the date my husband died and the date my son was born and know it's impossible. Todd didn't father Anders, but he's the only father he has ever known, even if it's only my memories. He doesn't ask questions. No one does. I suppose it's considered impolite to question a war widow."

I felt my mouth go dry. If she agreed with that ideal, then I was violating it. "I'm sorry for intruding. I under-stand your wishes, but I can't help but wonder why you took my father's money?"

I wanted to believe she was the woman she seemed to be, because it meant she was no threat to my family nor was her son. If that was true, I could respect her wishes and move on with my own life. But she had taken money and I could only assume it was for her silence.

"I debated whether or not to tell Albert," she explained. "In the end, I knew I had to leave. It was no secret that the two of us had become friends. If I stayed, there would be gossip and it wouldn't be long before the two of us were linked. I didn't want my pregnancy to become a scandal. I'm certain that people gossiped anyway. It wouldn't be the first time a woman disappeared from a domestic job. But it seemed the better of the two options, considering I wanted to keep the baby. Albert supported my decision. When I asked him to deny paternity, he agreed on one condition: he would be allowed to provide financial support for the child."

"So, he didn't pay you to keep quiet?" I asked.

"No. Children are expensive. You're a father now, so I suspect you know that. They need clothing and shoes and braces and schooling. Albert was adamant that his son not go without. In a way, I think he wanted to give Anders what he couldn't give you."

I tried to swallow this revelation but it lodged in my throat. My father had given me very little. Surely, she knew that. I couldn't quite ignore the twinge of jealousy this produced in me. "Approval? Love? I'm not sure you can send those with a monthly check."

"Your father often worried about the responsibility he would leave you. I'm not surprised that he gave his life to protect you. If he could have given you a choice, he would have."

This was news to me. My father had always loved the power his position afforded, it seemed to me. The idea that he somehow understood the personal sacrifice if required made me question everything. If my father had been the man Rachel claimed he was, then he was a stranger to me. But maybe that was what he wanted. How do you look your child in the eye and tell them that someday they will bear the weight of the world on their shoulders? I dreaded the day Elizabeth discovered the duty laid before her. Unlike my father, I would be behind her for as long as God allowed.

"Tell me about him," I requested in a soft voice. Rachel had made her wishes clear, and after I left here today I would respect them. Whether my father wanted to give Anders a life free from duty or not didn't matter. Not to me. I might never meet this man. But I could do him one service as his brother. I could forget about him. I could give him the life I would never have. Still, I couldn't quite do that without knowing who he was.

"He is responsible for this." She pointed to the gray in her hair, and despite the seriousness of our prior conversation, I laughed. "He's a daredevil. I think that a boy who grows up without his father has something to prove. He's awfully proud of Todd, but I wouldn't allow him to join the service. I like to think I'm a reasonable mother. I just couldn't stomach the thought of him on the front. He respected my wishes and took up motorcycle racing instead."

"I'm not certain that's any less dangerous," I pointed out. I couldn't help but think I might like him. I knew a thing or two about having something to prove. I also understood the rush of danger.

"It's not," she assured me. "I was the one who chose Silverstone, though. He grew up around it. At least he's crashed fewer bikes than cars."

"Is he married?" A wife might be the prescription he needed to finally settle down. It had been what healed me.

She shook her head, a sadness flitting over her features. "A mother can hope. Right now, he seems married to the road. I pray fate will intervene."

"It did in my case," I confessed. We sat there for another hour as she shared stories of schoolyard fights and car crashes. She painted a picture of a brother I had never known and would never know. At noon, I stood to take my leave.

Rachel saw me to the door. But before I could leave, I caught sight of a small table by the entry. A dozen framed photos clustered on it. The older ones I knew were of her husband. In a few, she was young and quite beautiful. No wonder she had caught my father's attention. Then there were the newer photos. I picked one up and stared. Anders and I shared the same eyes, but that was where the similarities ended. He was tall and broad shouldered with light blonde hair and an easy smile. In this photo the scruffy beginnings of a beard appeared on his jaw. In others, he was clean-shaven. But in all of them, he looked happy. I had never had family photos like this. My adolescence had been recorded by tabloids and newspapers. Rachel was right. My father had given him what he couldn't give me.

I placed the frame back on the table, and a strange wave of nostalgia swept over me. Perhaps, it was for a life I had never had. Turning to her, I gave her a hug.

"Watch out for him for me?" I asked her

She reached up and ruffled my hair. For a moment, a fleeting memory darted through my mind, but it was gone before I could latch on. "I always have."

159

That would be enough for a lifetime. It had to be. Anderson Stone might never know the truth, but that didn't mean he wasn't my brother. With her help, he didn't need to know. Taking one final look at the house, I left this family secret behind.

CHAPTER SEVENTEEN

It was his father's gun. He hadn't kept it for nostalgic reasons, although that would have been understandable. Smith had kept it with him during his employment with Hammond, and after he had been burned by his former employer, he had carried a single round with him.

He was saving it.

The day Brexton Miles showed up on his doorstep asking questions about Hammond's murder, Smith had shown him that bullet and explained its significance. He hadn't been the one to kill Hammond. Smith supposed it was some type of beautiful irony that the bullet he had saved to kill Hammond would now kill the man responsible for Hammond's death. He didn't act out of revenge. He knew he owed Hammond nothing.

Yes, Oliver Jacobson had left Smith and Belle alone for over a year. All signs pointed to the veracity of Hammond's claim that no one would come after him or his wife. But smith had learned a long time ago not to trust Hammond's word. Everything he touched, the man poisoned. In actuality, Smith had no idea where the conspiracy started. It was like a monster swallowing its own tail, never ending, never beginning, only a horror to behold.

He took Belle's car. The Mercedes was a slick, pretty ride for his wife—and it blended in on the London streets. In this town, a Merc was hardly noteworthy. Smith's Bugatti was an entirely different story. But he didn't leave the Veyron because it was flashy for a getaway car, though of course it was. Simply, if things went wrong, and he imagined they might, he wouldn't have a second thought about disposing of the little sports car.

If he had to choose between the Veyron and his life, he wasn't sure which one would survive.

He pulled into an open spot a few doors down from the address Georgia had given him and turned the car's lights off. It was too cold in London for him to sit in an unheated car and not fog up the windows. The important thing now was not to draw attention to himself.

Smith studied Jacobson's London townhouse and grimaced. He'd been privy to a brief rant straight from his enemy's lips about the privileged class. Apparently, Jacobson didn't hold himself to the same standards as those he preyed upon. Smith knew a thing or two about real estate, and it was easily worth a few million pounds.

"No reasoning with mad men." he said under his breath, as his fingers popped his collar up for added concealment.

He'd gone over the information that Georgia had given him a dozen times this evening, but now he ran through it again. Jacobson's family was in the country. Smith preferred it that way. The body would be found sometime around Christmas when he didn't arrive at the family estate, but not by his wife or children. Jacobson didn't deserve such consideration, but his family did. Some horrors a child could never unsee.

Smith's mind drifted to the swimming pool in the basement of his family's London home. He would never put a child through what he had been through, nor would he put his wife through what his mother had never been able to forget.

According to Georgia and her team of profilers, Jacobson was man of habit. When his wife and children were out of town, he'd retire for a pint at the local pub around 10:00pm. He'd stay for an hour before returning to his empty house. This was where Smith's plan deviated each time he considered it.

The rash side of him wanted to take Jacobson out at his first opportunity. He was ready to be done with this business, but he knew it might not be the best course of action. A far better plan would be to watch and wait for Jacobson to return home. If he did it on the street, there was the possibility it would be written off as a random act of violence. He could snatch Jacobson's wallet and make it look like a robbery. The only trouble was London itself. No city on earth had more surveillance cameras.

That left one final possibility. He could take care of

Jacobson in his home and do his best to keep his face obscured. The murder of a member of Parliament would be a national scandal. No matter who Smith's friends were, if he was fingered for the crime, he wouldn't be able to get out of it. He couldn't allow the fantasy of getting away with it to be part of his plan. If he was caught, he would take the blame. No one else.

Alexander would suspect there was more to it, but Smith doubted he would follow up on any inquiries into whether Georgia had shared classified intelligence. Once the King knew that Jacobson was responsible for the attacks on his family, any further interest in the case would disappear. Only one man would have to pay for the crime, and Smith had always been marked for something like this.

Like clockwork, the door to the townhouse opened and Jacobson ambled out in a corduroy field jacket and cap. For a man who claimed to hate the aristocracy, Jacobson didn't mind dressing like them, Smith noted with bemused detachment. Once Jacobson was well down the street, Smith got out of the Mercedes and locked it, then followed on foot. This hadn't been part of any of his plans, but instinct told him it was the right thing to do. He hung back as Jacobson entered the Horse and Hound, then he ducked in after him a few moments later. There were enough regulars in the place that no one seemed to notice a stranger in their midst. Smith took a table in the back corner, taking a page out of Georgia's book, and making sure his back was to the wall. Jacobson on the other hand, sat at the bar, and began a lively conversation with a half dozen or so men.

It was strange to see a predator in his natural habitat. Nothing about Jacobson's behavior belied how dangerous he truly was. It left Smith to wonder what was going on inside his head.

A barkeep wandered over, wiping his palms on the back of a bar towel tucked into his pocket. "Can I get you anything?"

"Scotch." Smith ordered, continuing his steep descent into old habits. The bartender tilted his head in acknowledgement and disappeared, reappearing a few moments later with his drink. Smith handed him a 100 pound bill. Tonight wasn't a night to use credit cards.

Jacobson chatted animatedly as he snacked on a basket of chips. "Enjoy that," Smith thought. It wasn't a proper last meal, but as his executioner, Smith didn't feel he owed him the courtesy.

A few minutes before 11:00, Jacobson raised his hand in the air to call for his bill, and Smith downed the rest of the drink he had been nursing. There would be no way to turn back after this.

He left the tavern before Jacobson had finished paying and returned to the Mercedes. Sliding into the driver's seat, he took the gun out of the glove box. Habit dictated he check the chamber. He knew there was only one round inside, but one was all he would need. There would be no hesitation, and there would be no mistake.

But as the chamber spun open, he found something he didn't expect.

The bullet was there, but where the rest of the rounds should have gone, tiny scraps of paper were lodged. He pulled the first out, recognizing Belle's handwriting immediately.

"If you're reading this," it said, "You think you no longer have choices."

She was right about that. He didn't have any other options not if he wanted to protect her. He withdrew the next slip and read it.

"If I'm not there to stop you, know that I will always trust your judgement."

He took out the next.

"If I'm waiting for you at home, come back to me, and let me help you find the light."

His hands began to tremble as he took out the last slip.

"You always have a choice."

The paper fell into his lap and he dropped the gun into the seat next to him. How could she have known? Or had she always suspected it would come to this?

Listening to her now meant abandoning the assurance Jacobson would never threaten her life again. But if he ignored her, he would refuse the most important request she'd ever made of him. "Come back to me." He could hear her voice saying it.

She could show him the light. Since the day he had met her, Smith had craved everything about her. He would give her anything. But could he step into the unknown with her?

He liked control. He clung to it. But he could never control everything.

Belle was waiting for him in Scotland. Belle, who believed in him, and in his ability to be a good man, even when he did not. Belle, who never questioned that, even when he revealed the darkness of his past. She had stood by his side. That was where he belonged now.

This was his choice, a future he couldn't predict. One that had far more beautiful possibilities than the ugly reality of his past. It was time for him to leave it behind. It was time for him to choose the man he would become, the man he already was.

He started the engine and pulled away from the curb just as Jacobson came into view. The man would never know how close he had come to dying that night, but Smith knew how close he had come to choosing the wrong path. He needed to find Belle and the light within her.

But first, he needed to speak to Alexander.

CHAPTER EIGHTEEN

S mith Price wasn't the sort of man to call at midnight for a chat. I had decided to return to my marital bed, only to be roused from it after a few minutes. My plan had been simple. Get some sleep and head to Scotland in the morning. I had promised Clara I would lay the issue of my brother to rest and then go to her. Now it seemed I was being called on to deal with an entirely different issue. It was a moment I had been dreading and anticipating for well over a year.

Shrugging on a simple black t-shirt, I didn't even bother to find trousers. If Smith had issues with seeing me in my boxers, that was a discussion for another day. My mobile rang on the bedside table, and I scrambled for it.

"I heard you have a visitor." Brexton didn't bother to greet me. Of course he would've been informed that an unknown party had shown up at the palace after hours.

"I do," I said tersely.

"Why is Smith Price coming to visit you?" Brexton asked. Apparently he wasn't going to beat around the bush. Normally, I appreciated his candor. Tonight I had more important things to consider.

"I'll let you know when I know," I promised him. Then I hung up before he could protest. I figured it was about four-to-one odds he would show up within the hour. I'd take those.

Padding into my study, I found Smith already waiting. He was still fully dressed, his hair damp from melting snowflakes. If I thought I hadn't been sleeping, he looked even worse. Bluish marks under his eyes betrayed him. Whatever he had come to tell me, he had known for a while. It had preoccupied him. But despite the weariness of his features, his eyes blazed. They sparked with a ferocity matched only by the fire that had been lit in the hearth. I waited for him to speak. As soon as the door clicked shut behind me, his mouth opened.

"Do we have him?" I asked.

Smith nodded, and it was all I needed to know. It hardly mattered who he was or why.

"Has he been arrested?" I asked. It was a stupid question. Why would Smith Price know that before I did?

But something had brought him here in the darkness to seek me out.

"No," Smith admitted. Then he withdrew a gun from his pocket. If any other man had done so in my presence, I would have rushed him, and tackled him to the ground before he could get off a shot. But although Smith Price and I didn't always see eye to eye, we understood each other.

He turned and set it on the mantle, then drew off his leather gloves. "Would you mind keeping that for me?"

"That depends," I said in a measured voice.

"It hasn't been used," Smith assured me, an answer to an unspoken question. "Not by me. Not for a long time."

"Do you always carry illegal firearms with you?" Of course a man like Price would. He'd seen the depraved side of London that most only imagined. He knew the nightmares and perversions were real, and he had something to protect.

"Why didn't you do it?" I asked him.

I knew why he was carrying the gun, and why he had brought it to me. It was part of why we understood each other. There was only one reason he would ever carry a pistol.

It was the same reason that part of me wanted to pick it up now. Smith had yet to name the man responsible for the murder of my father and the attacks on my wife, but I already wanted my hands around the man's throat. I wanted to watch him suffer. I wanted to watch him beg for his life, and then I wanted to take it from him. Perhaps I had been the wrong person to come to this evening, or maybe Smith had gone to the only person who could understand the contradictory nature of responsibility. My first impulse was to protect my wife, followed closely by the instinct for revenge.

Neither were luxuries I could afford.

"I saw the light," he said simply, as if this was explanation enough for him turning away from the task at hand.

I nodded. Whatever had lured Smith away meant something to him. I wouldn't ask him to share the intimate details of that, but I would ask him for the name. If I couldn't deliver my own personal brand of justice, I could bring the crown to his door.

"Oliver Jacobson," Smith told me. I searched my memory, looking for a connection I couldn't place.

"It's pathetic, really," Smith continued. "He's such a little man that we never even considered him.

"Parliament?" I asked. Brexton had indicated their sources had led them straight to the seat of power within London.

"Yes. I believe I was told he was a vocal minority," Smith said, as though he was recalling someone else's words.

"I hesitate to ask," I added, "But where did you get your information?"

"Do you really want to know?" he asked. "Is this an official inquiry?"

"Consider it off the books," I promised him.

"Our mutual acquaintance."

Smith didn't need to say more. We'd never discussed our own private involvement with Georgia Kincaid. Whether we were linked in more intimate ways hardly mattered now.

"You were right to tell me to look out for her," Smith said. "But not for the reason you think."

I cocked my head and waited. I'd ask Smith to keep an

eye on Georgia. Now I needed to know if she could be trusted.

"She came to me. She put the choice in my hands."

"I'm surprised she didn't do it herself," I said in a flat tone. Georgia was capable of it. It was one of the reasons I had hired her in the first place. She had been playing both sides then, and I'd never quite been sure who held her true allegiance. Now I knew it was the man in front of me, the last man I would've guessed.

"She thinks he did her a favor. He killed Hammond, after all. Hammond was always the monster in her closet." Smith's throat slid as if he was swallowing down a disgusting memory.

I knew the kind of perversion Georgia Kinkade craved. If Hammond had been the man to twist her, then I could never blame her for wanting him dead.

Somehow, Smith had walked away tonight. He was a smart enough man to get away with murder. *If* he had come to me in confession, I would have done my level best to help him conceal his involvement. But he had chosen another path, and I couldn't help but ask myself if I would have done the same.

My memories flashed to Clara, and the scent of burnt rubber mixed with rain and oil flooded my nostrils. We'd never been able to prove that the car accident was more than an accident, but after comparing it with several other cases, including the one that claimed Smith's first wife, I had no doubt that foul play was involved.

I could never forget collapsing in prayer over a twisted

hunk of metal on a rainy road. Some memories couldn't be erased, but they could be avenged. I glanced up and realized Smith was watching me with wary eyes.

"Georgia gave me the choice," he said in a strangled voice, "And it was difficult for me to walk away. I'm giving you that choice now."

It wasn't a coincidence that he brought a gun. He hadn't done it out of a dramatic need to show and tell about his evening. He was passing the job on to me. It was a show of respect and one I appreciated. I crossed to him and picked up the pistol. Spinning open the chamber, I noted there was only one copper bullet inside.

"It only—" Smith began.

"—takes one," I finished for him.

One shot, and Oliver Jacobson would be held accountable for the reign of terror he had begun. He thought he could play puppet master, but he never realized I was the one holding all the strings.

I held the gun in my hand, allowing the metal to warm to my touch. "I assume you have ample evidence."

"Georgia will show you profiles and notes from meetings. All sorts of *documentation*," Smith said. "But I met the man before tonight, and I can tell you, he's the one. I should have seen it then, but I was blind. I thought Belle and I were safe."

"What do you mean?" I ask.

He filled me in on the particulars of his mother-in-law's new neighbor, and my blood ran cold. The amount of time and effort Jacobson had put into planning this made me question if it would really end with him. He had found Hammond and his network of thugs and spies, and he had utilized them for his own gain. Even a bad guy sometimes grew a conscious. Smith Price was proof of that. I considered the weight of the pistol in my hand, staring at it for a long moment before placing it back on the mantle.

Smith had made a choice, and he did so out of personal duty to himself. I had even less flexibility in that regard. If Jacobson's intent had been to destroy the monarchy, choosing to take his life now might achieve his ends.

Instead, I went to my desk and picked up my mobile. Brexton answered on the first ring. "I want you to bring in Oliver Jacobson now," I ordered him. "No questions. Not until I see him."

I hung up the phone without waiting for his response. Then I went to the decanter of bourbon my father kept on the shelf and poured myself a glass. Raising it, I offered some to Smith.

He shook his head. "No thanks," he said. "I don't drink anymore."

THE CELL BREXTON had thrown Jacobson into was the sort of thing you expected to see in a movie. Governments like to tell you these places don't exist, but they do. They're for the use of men like me, and we reserve them for the worst kind of traitor.

Oliver Jacobson deserved even less. Not only had he betrayed the will of his country, and those he had been elected to serve, but he had betrayed the safety of my family. He thought I was a man bound by my own duty to British law. He'd soon learn that didn't extend to this place.

Smith had accompanied me against Brexton's wishes, but while my best friend had my interests at heart, he couldn't understand the ties that bound Smith and I together, not in this regard.

Jacobson had come without a fight. Perhaps due to good behavior, someone had bothered to give him a cup of tea. He sat in the dank cell, sipping it slowly as we entered. When he glanced up, he smiled as though we were all old friends meeting at the club. My hands curled into fists, but I did my best to remain in control.

"It's nice to see you again, Price," he said, acknowledging my companion. Jacobson looked utterly serene. He could have been having his conversation on a street corner. "It takes a little bit more than this to rile me up, I'm afraid."

"I wish I could say the same," Smith said flatly.

"Was that you this evening?" Jacobson asked. "At the pub, following me?"

I raised an eyebrow at Price, who shrugged.

"I have no idea what you're talking about." I did, but I kept this thought to myself. Giving Jacobson any information might prove dangerous if things began to go poorly.

"I am supposed to be spending Christmas with your mother-in-law," Jacobson continued conversationally. Next to me, Smith tensed. "It was disappointing to find out you wouldn't be there with your lovely wife. How is the beautiful Belle?"

"Don't say her name," Smith growled.

Before I could stop him, he'd lashed out, smashing his fist against the table and knocking over the hot tea.

"Is your temper going to come out to play, too?" Jacobson mocked me.

I grabbed Smith by the shoulder and helped him straighten up. Then I leaned in and lowered my voice. "Why don't you wait outside?" Smith had already faced his demons tonight. Asking him to do it twice might be too much.

He adjusted his jacket as he left, never turning around to look at the man who had been responsible for so much of the tragedy in his life.

"I suppose you want to ask me why," Jacobson continued as soon as Smith was out of the room.

There had been a time where I wanted that, but now I found it satisfying to know he'd never be free again. It hardly mattered why he did any of it. If I stayed on my best behavior, the audio and video recordings in the room could be used against him later. If I didn't stay on my best behavior, I'd have no problem using every power within my reach to keep him locked away. Either way, Oliver Jacobson would never be a free man again.

"Some of us weren't born with a silver spoon in our mouths," he said.

Apparently, he was going to tell me his sad story, regardless of whether or not I asked him to share it.

"There are those of us who weren't chosen in the lottery of birth, who've had to crawl our way out of the gutter, watching while men like you and your father abuse their power. I know everything about you, Alexander. I know the twisted secrets you keep in your closet. I know why you were sent off to the war."

"Yes, I was very privileged then," I said dryly. I crossed my arms and leaned against the wall. If he wanted to talk, let him. It occurred to me that Brexton might overhear something I had chosen to keep secret from him, but I could no longer afford secrets. Clara had shown me that. I had to learn to trust the people around me. That was the only way I was going to protect my family from men like him in the future.

"Daddy couldn't abide having a perverted son," Jacobson said, "And then he got stuck with a gay one. The lottery of birth, once again. But it never mattered when you sinned, did it? Never did a thing to earn your place, and yet you sit in judgment of me."

My eyes narrowed as I considered what he was saying. To be honest, I had expected more of him. There were questions I had, ones that would need to be answered in the coming weeks to ensure that the threat ended with him.

Perhaps after he told us more, we would understand how he had inspired the treachery of Hammond, but I suspected he simply bought it.

"You don't live in the gutter now," I pointed out. Smith had filled me in on more particulars about our suspect while we waited for Brexton to bring him in.

"As I said, I clawed myself free," he started, but I cut him off.

"Charles Dickens would be proud of you, but the rest of England has no patience for traitors."

"There are more like me," he warned. "Men who want to see the monarchy overturned, men who will enact legislation."

"Let them," I roared, losing my patience. "Do you want to talk about the lottery of birth? You claim to have been born in a gutter and to have fought your way to the top. That might have been admirable if you'd done so for the right reasons, but misplaced obsession only breaks a man."

I knew a thing or two about that, but I wouldn't bother to share it with this scum.

"It's easy for you to say," Jacobson began. "You've never had any choices."

"I have." I cut him off. "I chose to be a good man. You could've done the same. It's too late for that now, so I hope you rot in hell."

He began to talk wildly, but I was past the point of giving him any more of my time. He'd stolen precious moments from my life and from my family. He'd taken away things we could never have back, and I would never give him the satisfaction of a minute more. The heavy cell door groaned shut behind me.

Smith looked up from the floor, mouth opened, but I held my hand up before he could apologize. There was no need. He'd shown amazing restraint this evening. I couldn't hold it against him when he yelled at the man.

"What now?" Smith asked. "Now we lock him up and we throw away the key," I told him, "And then we go home."

"You are home," Smith pointed out.

"Neither of us are home." I shook my head at the absurdity of the thought. "Our homes are in Scotland with our wives."

CHAPTER NINETEEN

*I*t was Christmas Eve. Guests would be arriving any minute, and David wasn't speaking to him.

It had taken Edward an embarrassingly long time to realize his fiancé was hiding. Once he began to search for him he quickly began to panic. It had been a long time since David ran away, but he'd always had good cause to do so before.

Edward had asked a lot of him in the early years of their relationship. Whereas David had never needed to hide his sexuality, he had done so to protect Edward. Now, once again, Edward had managed to drive him away, and he didn't know why. It didn't help that Balmoral had dozens of rooms for David to abscond to. Checking them all might take the rest of the day. While it might be considered rude not to greet his guests, he wasn't about to spend Christmas without his love.

An hour later he'd checked half of the house and panic

was subsiding into frustration. The sound of movement in the west library caught his attention, and he doubled back to check the space again. David didn't bother to hide when Edward entered the room. Instead, he glanced up from a book and frowned.

"I've been looking for you everywhere." Edward spread his hands in concern, but it didn't vanquish the displeasure on David's face.

"I was reading," he said shortly.

"I can see that." Edward willed himself to find a reserve of patience he hadn't yet tapped.

David had never been as comfortable around large groups as Edward was, but he couldn't avoid them forever, not if he wanted to marry into this unusual, dysfunctional family.

"I'm not avoiding guests," David explained to him, "I'm avoiding you."

That was a bad sign. Edward considered his options, finally deciding to take the seat across from David. "And why is that?"

"Don't you have guests to attend to?" David asked.

"No one is more important than you." Edward tried to sound reassuring, but this only seemed to ratchet up the tension between them.

"No one?" David repeated. "Not Belle or Clara?"

Edward's eyebrows furrowed in confusion. "They're here to help with the wedding."

"I'm here to help with the wedding," David cut him off, "But I've barely seen you the last few days."

"I'm sorry. I guess I wanted everything to be perfect." Edward knew it wasn't an excuse, and from the looks of it David wasn't going to let him off the hook so easily.

"And I just wanted to be with you. That's what this is supposed to be about. We said no big wedding. Remember?" David prompted.

He tossed his book on a nearby end table and sighed.

"This is about us," but even Edward couldn't bring himself to believe it. He had been focused on the cake and the flowers. He had poured over the words he wanted Alexander to use when he married them, and he'd been making quiet trips into the village to procure supplies. *I wanted to give you a wedding,* that was what he meant to say.

David deserved one.

He had certainly waited for one.

"I only ever asked for an 'I Do,'" David reminded him. He stood, moving to leave the room, but Edward grabbed his hand.

"Don't go," he urged, "Allow me to apologize properly for being a wanker."

"I'm not sure there are enough words in the English language for that apology," David said, but he paused.

He didn't pull out of Edward's grip. Instead, their hands remained linked.

"Am I really that bad?" Edward asked.

"Sometimes when Clara and Belle are around," David told him. "When they are you go into girlfriend mode. It makes me jealous."

"Jealous of Clara and Belle?" Edward said incredulously.

"Well, I don't think you're going to run off with them," David's response was dry, but Edward spotted the hurt in his eyes, "You do leave me out though."

"I guess we leave all the men out." Edward held up his hands. "I'm not trying to make an excuse. I'm just trying to understand."

A flicker of a smile betrayed David. "So, I'm the man then?"

"Of course, you are," Edward said, "I'm the one who likes dresses, after all."

David groaned, but before he could come back with another retort Edward stood and pressed his lips to his. "Tell me when I'm being a prick," Edward commanded.

"Notice when I'm being a loner," David suggested.

"You know, I'm told that marriage isn't easy," Edward said, "But I think it will be worth it if you are by my side."

They had encountered rough waters before. There had been storms that nearly tore them apart, but somehow, they had clung together. That's how they survived.

"I couldn't live without you," Edward whispered.

"I just want to live with you," David said gently.

"You are my everything," Edward promised. "And I'm going to give you the world."

David brushed a kiss over his lips. Then he pulled back, grinning impishly, "Anything?"

"Anything," Edward repeated, despite the alert bells ringing inside him.

David grabbed his other hand and pulled him close. "Good, because I'd love to talk about a baby."

CHAPTER TWENTY

I strode into Balmoral Castle like I owned the place, which in point of fact, I did. Unlike my other homes, Balmoral belonged to my family rather than being given to me in trust of my title. Norris met me at the door but he was too late to stop my entry.

"You're getting soft," I informed him good-naturedly.

His head cocked to the side. "You—if you don't mind me saying so—are less paranoid."

"It's a new day," I informed him.

As a matter of fact, it was Christmas Eve. I had made good on my promise to Clara. I would spend Christmas with my wife and daughter. Now I just needed to find them.

Signs of Edward's penchant for decor were all around. The entire castle looked like a Christmas village had been blown up and its remnants scattered throughout. I didn't wait for Smith to follow behind me. We'd traveled together mostly in silence as we contemplated the events of the last day, but instead of tension, the atmosphere had been one of relief. We both knew we had our entire lives ahead of us and our wives waiting for us in Scotland.

Mrs. Watson met me as I passed the kitchen, wiping her hands on an apron, then throwing them around me. "I was wondering when you would get here, sir."

"Do not call me sir," I ordered her. I was fairly certain this woman had changed my nappies, but pride kept me from bringing that up.

"There's so much going on," she explained. "But first, young Edward wants to speak with you."

"And I to him," I said absently. "But first, tell me where my wife is."

"They'll be in the parlor with the wee one."

I pulled away from the old housekeeper, kissing her on the cheek before I left. "Tell me she isn't the prettiest thing you've ever seen," I called over my shoulder.

"The prettiest," Watson confirmed.

I paused in the doorway and took in the scene before me. The Christmas tree was lit, crowded around the base with so many presents that I couldn't imagine where we would put them all—and I lived in a palace. The fire crackled in the hearth, warming the room and casting it in a heavenly glow. This was exactly where I needed to be.

I saw that now.

It had taken me far too long to get here. I had seen to my work and nothing would ever stand between me and my family again. Clara was in the middle of the chaos, her arms wrapped around Elizabeth as she held her up to everyone's delight.

"There aren't nearly enough babies in this scene," I announced in a booming voice. The conversation died down.

Madeline Bishop looked up from her granddaughter. She was a gorgeous, older woman with wavy chestnut hair like her daughters. I imagined Clara would be like that someday. I only hoped she was less high-strung. She called over to me, "Whose fault is that?"

"No one's but my own," I admitted. Striding across the room, I stole my daughter from Clara's arms. Kissing her on the forehead, I passed her off to Belle, who took her with a natural ease. I paused, eying her momentarily. Later on, I'd have to study her for signs. She might be good for bringing more babies into the Christmas scene next year. Regardless, I had plans on filling that need on my own.

Bending down, I took Clara's hand and drew her quickly to her feet. "I think I'll see to it now," I said. Then I scooped her over my shoulder and carried her off. She was too surprised to protest, even as everyone around us began to laugh.

As soon as we hit the hallway, she began to pound on my back. "Put me down. This is undignified."

"Want me to list all the undignified things we've done in our relationship? I can do that, or I can take you upstairs."

She melted at the suggestion, the fight going out of her body. Apparently, I had been right to assume that my wife wanted to see me. We only made it to the private corridor that led to our bedroom before I lost my patience. I lowered Clara to her feet.

"Do you remember the first time you met my family?" I asked her.

She grimaced at the unpleasant memory. "I do."

I caught her hips in my hands and began to slide the fabric of her skirt up to her waist. "Do you remember what happened after?"

"I remember that you gave me some excuses about your compulsions." Fire danced in her blue eyes, and I couldn't stop myself from kissing her. She responded with her body, pressing herself against me as I hooked my thumbs in her knickers and pushed them to the ground.

I couldn't get enough of her. I never would. But, God help me, that wouldn't stop me from trying. Pulling away, I lingered, my lips a breath away from her own. "I told you that some compulsions are healthy."

"Not all of them," she protested, even as she fought to get closer to me.

"This is," I murmured. I dipped my hand between her legs, my fingers spreading her cunt. "Spread wider, poppet."

There was no hesitation. We might need to work on our communication in other avenues, but sex was a language we spoke fluently. Clara responded to my touch as wantonly as the first time we met. I might never give her everything she needed, but I would try—and I would never fail where it came to her body.

"You can't control me," she whimpered, but she didn't

187

protest as I brought my free hand to her stomach and held her against the wall. If that's what she thought this was about then I needed to clarify a few things.

"It's not about control. Not this. Not now." I trailed my lips along her ivory jaw, writing my promises in breath against her skin. "I'm compelled to give you pleasure. I'm willing to compromise everywhere else, but I will fuck you. I will make love to you. I will take you to the edge and hold you as you spill over. Ecstasy is what I demand of you. I can't quiet my need to give it you. It is a healthy compulsion."

Her response hitched in her throat, a strangled mewl of longing escaping past her lips. Finally, she managed two, small words. "Yes, please."

I didn't need her permission, and I wouldn't ask for it. Not when it came to making her come. Watching Clara writhe with pleasure, helpless to resist, was my oxygen. The rest of my life was spent holding my breath until the next time I could gasp for air again. I could compromise on every other issue. I would strive to be the man she deserved and one that she could trust. She would be protected and respected in my arms. But she could never deny this need.

Trailing kisses up her naked thighs, I savored each one as I worshipped her body. I would give her my devotion just as I had given her my life. I slid my tongue slowly to the hollow between them, and her hands tangled in my hair. Her reaction took me back to that night in the hall. I had barely known her then, but I was already her captive.

Drawing the tip of my tongue along the wet heat of her seam, I felt my cock twitch with impatience. He would have to wait, because I was exactly where I wanted to be.

"Let go, poppet," I urged, her scent flooding my nostrils as I spoke. "I'm going to fuck you with my mouth. I need to taste you as you come."

She inhaled sharply as if bracing herself, and I thrust my tongue inside her. I stroked hard only pausing on her delicious clit. Her fingers tightened their grip on my hair, and she began to shake. Wrapping my arms around her legs, I held her against me as I continued my assault. She didn't hold back as she came, her arousal gushing against my mouth. When she tried to pull away, I didn't let go. Instead, I idled there, brushing kisses along her trembling cunt.

Finally, she released my head, but she didn't break away. "I need to feel you inside me."

I was on my feet with her in my arms instantly. She sagged against me, her face tucked below my chin so that I could feel the soft heat of her breath. Kicking the door closed behind us, I lowered her to her feet. When she took a shaky step toward me, my arms were waiting to catch her. "Let me help you, poppet."

She clung to me as I lifted her skirt up and drew her dress over her head. Abandoning it to the floor, I studied her body appreciatively. It wasn't the same as when we first met, this body was more beautiful, softened by motherhood and ripened by cultivation. I brought my hands to her breasts and skimmed over them, pausing to flick her nipples. They hardened into two beads that I couldn't resist. Slanting my head, I sucked a mouthful between my lips and Clara cried out. Moving to the other I couldn't help but toy with her. "I could make you come like this with my tongue and my teeth."

"I think you just proved that," she complained through gritted teeth.

"I was willing to prove it again, but..." The back of my head was shoved closer, and I chuckled.

"More," she demanded as I nipped the delicate furls.

I couldn't wait any longer to fulfill her request. Cupping her ass, I lifted her so she could wrap her legs around my waist.

"Slowly," I cautioned her as her sex nudged against the broad crown of my cock. It was as much a reminder to myself as it was to her. I had to fight the impulse to plunge inside her. Even after all this time, her entrance strained to accommodate me. She glided down my shaft, her cunt rippling against the engorged flesh. But it wasn't enough. I needed more. I longed to be brutally deep inside my wife. Moving toward the bed, I lowered our bodies slowly, never breaking our union.

Clara brushed a strand of hair away from her eyes, and our gazes met. We stayed like that, seeing into one another's souls, as I rocked myself fully inside her. Clara's head tipped back and she struggled to maintain the visual contact as she began to unravel. It was the most beautiful vision in the world—her porcelain body quivering uncontrollably. She bit down on her lower lip, sobs pouring from her, as she came. Her cunt clamped against me, drawing forth my orgasm in punctuated spasms, until I emptied inside her.

I held her for a few minutes or a few hours, her body clutched to mine. We laid in silence, the only movement a brush of the fingers or a soft, fleeting kiss. When I finally withdrew, I watched mesmerized as my seed spilled from her swollen pink mound.

"Everything I am belongs to you," I promised her in a whisper.

"Forever?" she asked, her eyes shining with unshed tears.

"For always."

CHAPTER TWENTY-ONE

*C*lara snuggled against his chest, releasing a deep sigh of contentment. This was where she belonged. No matter how stubborn she acted or the hoops she made him jump through, she was Alexander's. She had been from the moment she saw him in the lounge at the Oxford and Cambridge Club. Despite her desire that day to write him off as a bad boy, she had been drawn to him, inexplicably so. And nothing had ever been the same since. One brief moment, one stolen kiss and everything had changed. Clara had had a plan for her life and he had come along to upset the destiny she had laid out for herself.

She ran her palm over the slab of muscles that comprised his abdomen, her fingers pausing along the scars that snaked over his torso. Once he had hidden himself from her, showing her only glimpses of the darkness of his past and the burdens he carried inside him.

Sometimes he regressed into those habits and it was her job to bring him back to the light. He caught her hand, grasping it with his and lingered over the scars. They were physical reminders of the accident that claimed his sister's life and set him on a trajectory toward her.

"You don't have to," he said, hesitantly.

She wriggled her fingers free and brushed along the damaged tissue. "I want to. I want all of you, X. The beautiful and the ugly. The darkness and the light."

"You already have it," he vowed to her.

She rolled over and climbed on top, straddling his trim waist. Placing her hands over the scars, she rocked her hips until they made contact with his thickening cock. She kept her hands there as the two found each other naturally. His crest knocked gently at her entrance and she lifted herself just high enough to grant him access. Then Clara enveloped him slowly, losing herself to the sensation as he stretched delicate tissues.

In the past, Alexander had been too much for her. He brought too much emotion, too much pain, too much of him for her to handle. Now she accepted the beauty of their bittersweet relationship. She would never have enough of him—physically and spiritually. He completed her. Within her there was a void only he could fill.

Alexander's hands closed over hers as he began to roll his hips in a steady, quickening rhythm.

"Be with me," he called to her. "I want to see how beautiful you are when you're riding my cock."

She opened her eyes to find his trained on hers. As the first, white-hot emissaries of climax stole through her limbs, she cried out, riding through the fire under his lustful gaze. But before she could collapse against him, Alexander's hands found her hips and provided the endurance she no longer had. Her body fought her, as her heart once had, but neither answered to her will any longer. When the friction built again, she exploded, taking him with her.

Clara flopped against the pillow in a boneless heap of limbs. Satiated didn't begin to describe how she felt. Clutching the sheet to her chest, she shot a mischievous glance at her husband.

"It's been a while," she said breathlessly. Clara had grown accustomed to their daily lovemaking. Actually, most of the time, it was damn near hourly. It had been far too long since he had last taken her to bed and now she felt used and strained and sore—all in the best way possible.

"Ten days," he informed her.

"Did you count the minutes, too?" she asked, cocking an eyebrow at him. Trust it to Alexander to know how long he'd gone without claiming her body. She couldn't help taking a little pleasure in knowing that he had missed her as much as she had missed him.

"Speaking of, we need to catch up," he said, propping himself onto his elbow and casting his eyes upon her. "Is there something you want to tell me?"

Alexander's gaze pierced through her, and Clara bit her lip, grinning sheepishly. "Maybe."

It was pointless to hedge. From the looks on his face, he already knew, but his acknowledgement was the first true confirmation she had received. Her suspicions had begun to grow in the last few days but she'd been far too busy to see them through. Alexander reached over and circled her nipple with his fingertip lazily. Even the slight touch set her on edge. He was teasing, or rather, testing her body, and her response might have proven his theory.

"Well," he prompted, "how far along are you?"

She resisted the urge to pull the sheet over her head.

"I don't know," she whispered, daring an embarrassed grin instead.

"You don't know?" he repeated. "This sounds like a familiar story."

"I've been a little busy." Defensiveness overcame her. It wasn't as if she had planned this, and he was the reason she'd been distracted anyway. Maybe he needed a reminder of that. "And I was mad at you."

"That doesn't change the fact that you're pregnant, poppet." Alexander's hand slid to cover her belly and laid his palm flatly against the soft tissue that would soon swell with life.

"For all I know, you *just* got me pregnant." She informed him but with Alexander there to face facts, she knew that wasn't the case. The mood swings, the irritability, and the incessant urge to cry constantly, it was all there. Even Belle had bothered to point it out which made Clara wonder if her best friend suspected before she did.

"Even I'm not that skilled. Though it hurts to admit it."

"How did you know anyway?" Clara asked. She'd had every reason to be upset with Alexander in London, so if he tried to pin it on that, he had another thing coming. No, Alexander hadn't been privy to the emotional gymnastics she'd put on for Belle and Edward. If he had guessed, there had been some other clue she was missing.

He pressed his lips into a bemused smile and shook his head. "No way."

"Now you have to tell me," she cried, picking up a pillow and beating him with it.

He released a tortured sigh before he tilted his head and admitted his source. "I can taste it."

Clara blinked, trying to process this confession. "I'm not certain that's a good thing."

"It is." A smug smile carved over his handsome features. Not for the first time, she hoped the baby looked like him with his inky black hair and crystal blue eyes. *There were worse things than carrying the child of a human sex god who worshiped you*, she thought, *even if he could be an arrogant prick sometimes.*

Her hand found the one resting on her belly and she covered it, holding him there in that sacred spot. Alexander's eyes closed, a reverent calm overcoming his features, as if he was holding vigil.

"Happy Christmas," Clara whispered. Then a terrible thought occurred to her. She hadn't bought him a single present. She couldn't help but wonder if she should plead hormonal insanity in the morning or confess now. "I have to warn you, I don't have anything to give you."

He popped one eye open, then the other and the love reflecting from them nearly blinded her. "Clara, you've given me everything."

COMPLETE ME

CHAPTER TWENTY-TWO

The entire family was gathered into the parlor that evening. Their number had doubled throughout the course of the day, and now they were complete. It was an odd mish-mash of people and a few they suspected might show, like Alexander's grandmother or his friend, Brexton, were nowhere to be found.

But Belle's heart was full. She had spent plenty of Christmas Eves drowning her sorrows with a stolen bottle of wine while avoiding her mother. Last year had been the first holiday that she had not spent at the Stuart family estate. Now getting to spend her Christmas Eve with the people she cherished most, she knew that breaking that tradition had been the right choice.

In the past, she had been desperate for her mother's approval. She'd sought it by agreeing to a marriage that would bolster their family standing and ensure the financial security of Stuart Hall. Now Belle chalked it up to being young and foolish. She knew it ran deeper than that, though. She had wanted to be loved and, without understanding what that really meant, she had been willing to overlook how people like her mother and Philip treated her in return for the illusion of it. When she had ended things with her ex-fiancé, it took her a long time to accept that some people didn't change.

As a girl, she had wanted to believe that if she did the things her mother asked, she would be loved in return. Now as she looked around this room full of people who had been there for her through every up and down, a firm conviction settled over her. She'd heard it said before, but now she truly understood what it meant to choose her own family. They were an imperfect bunch, to be sure, but they were hers and she wouldn't give them up for anything.

Elizabeth crawled over and used Belle's knees to pull herself into a standing position.

"Clever girl," Belle praised, picking her up under her arms and placing the baby in her lap. "You take after your auntie."

Holding her, Belle knew that accepting nothing less than loyalty and unconditional love was her destiny to claim. That seemed a particularly important realization to come to as she considered the leap into motherhood.

Elizabeth caught a lock of her blonde hair and tugged on it, trying to pull it toward her mouth. Belle shook her head, clucking softly and maneuvered it away, only to have Elizabeth catch her palm. The baby seemed content to try to put that in her mouth instead.

Belle couldn't help but laugh as joy flooded through her. When she felt eyes burning across the room, she lifted her own to find Smith watching her with the baby through hooded eyelids. He drank in the sight before him, which was something Belle didn't mind doing herself.

Her husband had opted to dress down in a charcoal sweater and a pair of jeans. He didn't usually wear things that were so casual, and she made it a point to let him know exactly how she felt about the way his ass looked in those pants. As soon as they returned to London, there was going to be a whole new drawer of jeans waiting for him.

His gaze didn't waver from her. Even from a distance, she could see the fierce desire in his emerald eyes. Heat creeped under her cheeks as she recalled welcoming him to Balmoral earlier this afternoon.

It had been easy to slip away, given Alexander's boisterous entrance. Smith had caught her attention from the doorway, and while everyone laughed as Clara was carried off to her bedroom, Belle and Smith made their way to theirs.

"You're here," she whispered as soon as they were alone.

"There's something I have to tell you." He dropped her hand and paced the length of the room. Her heart leapt into her throat. She'd worried that there was a reason he had insisted on staying behind in London. It couldn't be a coincidence that he was grappling with guilt now.

"Tell me," she pressured him.

"I saw Georgia," he began, but when she opened her

mouth to ask questions, he stopped her. "Let me finish. She had information about the man who killed Hammond."

"Whoever killed Hammond did us all a favor," Belle said coldly. She could spare no remorse for a man who had never showed her an ounce of humanity. He had been a monster and they were better off with him gone.

"You and Georgia are so alike," he muttered, but when Belle's eyes narrowed, he hurriedly took it back.

Belle sensed her husband needed to confess, and she would gladly absolve him. She trusted him to do what was right for both of them, even if her heart raced with apprehension. "Did you kill him?"

"I turned him in," he said to Belle's surprise. "I found your notes—in the gun."

She had placed them there on instinct. Smith had given her so much. If the only thing she ever granted him in return was the faith to believe in choice, she might be able to repay him.

There would be a time to ask for particulars, but she wouldn't force him to process all of his feelings at once. Instead, she began to unbutton her blouse. Smith moved to face her and followed suit. They didn't touch each other as they undressed. Instead, they stripped slowly until they stood with nothing between them.

He would have done it—for her. The thought that this man would kill to protect her was almost as hot as the fact that he didn't. If he had any doubt about his choice, she would erase it by placing her body in his hands.

EDWARD DROPPED onto the couch beside her, interrupting her daydream.

"You're looking rather heated," he pointed out. "Do I need to turn down the boiler or is this something that can't be helped?" Belle's eyes flickered to her husband, and Edward groaned. "That's what I thought."

"Just wait," she warned him. "You're about to be in your honeymoon period. Then no one will be able to stand to be around you either."

"I hope so," Edward said good-naturedly, giving her a wink over the rim of his glasses. "How did we get so lucky, anyway?"

He had found David across the room and his face was a mixture of love and longing as he studied him.

"I have a favor to ask you," Belle said, tearing her eyes away from Smith. Edward drew in a deep breath, before he nodded. She suspected he would understand what she was asking. "I need you to make more room in your life."

Edward's gaze dropped to her stomach as if his glasses could be used as a sonogram. "Smith works fast," he said with a chuckle.

Belle elbowed him in the ribcage. "I want you to make room for Smith."

She didn't bother to add that with any luck, he'd need to be making a little more room in the future as well.

Edward glanced to David. "I'd like you to do the same."

The two of them had been best friends and while their allegiance would always be to one another, it was becoming increasingly clear that their husbands would be part of their lives forever. Belle didn't want Edward to feel as if he had to choose between Belle and becoming Smith's friend. As far as she was considered, Smith was as permanent an addition to her life as her right arm.

"I think your husband's ears are burning," Edward said as Smith prowled across the room toward them. Belle felt a rush of anticipation thrill through her.

"Take Elizabeth?" she asked.

"Excuse me," Smith interrupted them as Belle handed the baby to Edward, "but I'd like to steal my wife away. I think it's time she heads to bed."

Belle didn't miss the way Edward's eyes rolled a little. Smith's insatiable libido was something he was just going to have to get used to.

Smith took her hand, guiding her through the corridors to their private bedchamber. When they entered, he didn't flip on the light switch.

"You were serious about going to bed?" Sleep was usually the last thing on her husband's mind when he suggested they retire for the evening.

There was only enough moonlight to make out the silhouettes of furniture inside the room, but after a moment her eyes adjusted. Smith stayed close to her. All that mattered was that she could see him, even cast in shades of gray.

"I have something for you." He led her to the bed and handed her a box tied with a long, red ribbon.

"That's not what I was expecting," she said under her breath.

"You'll get that, too, beautiful," he promised her.

She plucked free the ribbon and lifted the lid of the box. Inside, hundreds of feathers cushioned a small black machine. "I knew it was too big to be diamonds," she had teased, "But I'm not sure what this is."

"I have something for you tomorrow," he promised her. "Tonight, you get stars."

He lifted the machine free and flipped the switch. Instantly, a dazzling array of light shimmered across the room, covering the ceiling with constellations. It reminded her of New York and wedding rings and promises made. He had given her the stars then and he was doing so again now.

She cleared her throat, her voice thick with emotion. "I thought I was on the naughty list."

Smith placed the machine on the table and fingered the untied ribbon. "That can be arranged, beautiful. Turn around."

His mouth swept across the arch of her neck and he undressed her. When she was nude, he guided her onto her stomach. His palms flattened on her ass, spreading her to him. She wiggled her legs open, but instead of dipping between them, he picked up each of her wrists and brought them behind her back. A moment later the silky ribbon from her present slid around them, cinching them tightly together. He continued playing with it for a moment.

"You look so pretty, tied in a bow for me." He bent over her to whisper in her ear. "Can I play with my toy now?"

"Yes, Sir," she breathed.

"You are on the naughty list," he informed her, his hand rubbing circles over her ass. "Aren't you?"

He prompted her answer with a firm, stinging smack.

"Yes, Sir."

"It so happens that I prefer the naughty list." This revelation was followed by a quick series of whaps to her bottom that left the tender flesh singing with sensual pain. "Your ass is as red as this bow, beautiful."

He slid a finger down the crack between her cheeks and she writhed under the gentle touch. She wanted more. Since they'd begun to try for a baby, most of their love-making had been purely traditional. Belle's preferences, however, ran the gamut.

"Please, Sir," she begged.

"You're dripping for me," he told her. A moment later, she felt the blunt crest of his cock massaging along her seam. "I've been saving this for our future."

"Oh." She couldn't bite back the disappointment. Part of her needed the primal, taboo side of Smith. But she wouldn't say no to him any way she could have him. Smith surprised her, though, bending over to run a tongue along the sensitive pink rosebud. Belle clenched at the contact but relaxed as he continued to circle leisurely.

After a few minutes, a finger pushed inside and began to pump.

"It's Christmas," Smith said with a groan, "I'll give you both."

With a gentle slowness, he guided his dick into her, until he hit resistance. Then he pulled out and did the same. His finger continued the assault of her tight hole and Belle's legs began to shake.

"I love seeing you filled with me," Smith growled, increasing his pace until she shattered beneath him. His warmth flooded inside her and she groaned as he pulled out slowly. His fingers brushed the seed dripping from her upward. He smeared it over the pink circle. "Is this what you want?"

He nudged against the tight pucker, giving her a moment to process the idea. Belle didn't have a safe word. She had never wanted one with Smith, and she never needed it. He knew her body's responses like his own. She circled against the tip in invitation. Smith inched within gradually, giving her body time to adjust. His hands tightened on her hips when he slid in entirely.

They had spent the afternoon making love. There was only one thing on her mind now.

"Fuck me," she begged, her hips beginning to writhe against him.

"I'm sorry?" He didn't move, and she knew exactly what he wanted to hear.

"Fuck me, Sir."

Smith pulled back and thrust inside her with one smooth jab. The sensation was utterly different, and it never ceased to make her feel wanton. In his presence, she was shameless, existing only for his pleasure. That libidinous exchange of power had always guaranteed the same would be returned to her.

"I love fucking your ass, beautiful," he growled as he

continued to plunge. He grabbed her tied wrists and jerked until her back arched in the air. Belle craned her neck so see her husband, wanting him to see the ecstatic contradiction of pain and pleasure that consumed her. She felt her eyes rolling back as the first wave crashed over her, dragging her under. He continued to thrust until she went limp.

Belle was barely aware as he untied her wrists and massaged the indentations the ribbon had left. He scooped her up and repositioned her on the bed. A few minutes later, a warm, wet towel wiped along her singing sex. She nearly howled at the contact, her body still overly sensitive, and she saw him bite back a grin.

"Don't look so please with yourself," she whispered sleepily.

"I can't help it. You look so pretty with your red cheeks," he told her, climbing onto the bedside beside her. At some point, he had undressed. She felt a twinge of disappointment that she hadn't seen it. But when he cradled her body to his, it evaporated. "I think I'd have to stop screwing you entirely to not look pleased. Giving you orgasms is one of my greatest accomplishments."

"Promise not to stop?" Her eyes were becoming heavy, but as sleep lured her under, she heard his quiet response.

"I promise. Forever."

CHAPTER TWENTY-THREE

*I*f Christmas Eve had been a warm, family gathering, Christmas morning was a frenetic mess of activity. Wads of paper littered the floor from gift wrapping, presents were piled next to each person, and, to Mrs. Watson's horror, plates of food had been sneaked into the parlor.

The Bishop clan hadn't acted like strangers for long. They had made themselves at home almost immediately. That included waiting until everyone was in bed and bringing in enough gifts to nearly double the collection at the base of the tree.

"We'll still be opening presents next Christmas," Lola grumbled under her breath. As soon as she opened her box to reveal an Alexander McQueen clutch, she squealed with delight. "Thank you, Mum!"

Madeline gazed fondly at her younger daughter. "I saw

it and knew you had to have it. It's harder to shop for clothes for you these days."

She cast a pointed glance at Lola. Then directed it at Belle Stuart.

"Don't look at me," Lola said. "It was all her idea. I caved to peer pressure." She winked at her business partner. Leave it to the Bishops to complain about not being able to spend more money.

Despite Madeline's success with a start-up web company, she didn't understand the need for Bless. Why would women rent what they could buy? Lola didn't try to explain that not everyone had their bank accounts.

Harold hadn't left his wife's side all morning. The holidays had brought them closer than ever, and playing the part of good old St. Nick seemed to bring a joy to the couple that they hadn't shared for a long time.

Clara watched them across the room, warmth spreading through her chest. She had tried to stay out of her parents' affairs—or rather, her father's affairs—but it hadn't always been easy. She knew better than anyone though that marriages had to be fixed from within. Both parties had to make it want to work in order for there to be compromise and cooperation. Her parents had stayed together this long. She could only that their new-found companionship blossomed into the romance they had once shared.

Alexander appeared at her side and followed the direction of her sight. Then he placed his arm around her, pulling him closer to him. Elizabeth babbled on her mother's hips, still in a plaid sleeper from last night. The two had decided to keep their Christmas surprise a secret for a little while longer. But he couldn't help but grin as he thought of Madeline Bishop's welcome to him the day before. If more grandchildren was what she wanted, he would be happy to oblige.

If only every day could be like Christmas, he thought. Seeing the peace on his wife's face and the giddiness overwhelming his daughter made him wish he could spirit them both away to the Scottish countryside and spend every morning like this.

"We'll need another room to put all of her toys in," Clara said dryly.

"Imagine how bad it will be next year," he whispered. He had yet to decide if he hoped to buy a train set or a doll next year. With any luck, he would get to do both. Twins had run in the Royal family in generations past.

Clara's eyes narrowed as she watched the gears turn in his head. "What are you plotting, X?"

"My Christmas present," he told her in a lowered voice.

A rosy flush heated her cheeks. "What about my Christmas present?"

"You can unwrap that later," he reassured her with a smug smile.

It was his signature crooked grin. The one that had caught her attention the day they met and the one that had held it after subsequent day after. She wanted to kiss that smirk right off his face, but she knew where that would lead. After last night, she was still exhausted.

"Actually," he said, lifting a small box he'd been hiding in his other hand, "I did get you something."

But Clara's eyes didn't fall on the actual present, they zeroed in on the ivory envelope on top that had been sealed with red wax stamped with the letter *X*. If it was anything like the notes he used to send her, its contents weren't family friendly.

"Maybe I should open that later."

"Open it now." He reached for Elizabeth.

Stepping to the side, so that she was out of sight, she slid her index finger under the flap, breaking the seal, and withdrew the handwritten note inside.

POPPET,

I've been remiss at sending you these little notes. I took for granted having you next to me and forgot the need to romance you. I told myself once that if I ever got the chance to reclaim your heart I would never let a day go by without earning it. I've failed at that. But from this day forward I am going to prove my commitment to you and our children.

CLARA SWALLOWED BACK the tears that were creeping into her throat. But it was as if Alexander had suspected this might happen, because as the note continued it shifted from sentimental to sensual.

211

You should also know that I don't plan to let ten days go by without worshipping your body. I realize that might be difficult, considering your condition, but I'm willing to try. My hands. My cock. My mouth. They exist to serve your pleasure, and I will spend every day for the rest of my life to touch, to lick, to bite, to suck, to kiss, and to make love to you.

For always,

X

"You can open your present now," he told her huskily.

Clara gasped at the sudden interruption. His words had taken her to another place, and she needed a second to recover. Tearing open the paper, she found a long jewelry box. She flipped open the lid to discover a stunning ruby bracelet. The gems were held in place by criss-crossing slashes of gold. They formed tiny *x's* all the way around. It was a message: X was reclaiming his territory.

"Help me put it on," she whispered. It took a moment, given that Elizabeth decided to help her parents out. But when it was safely clasped, Clara studied it. "It's perfect."

"So are you." He brushed a kiss over her forehead.

"Have you ever seen such a disgusting display of affection?" Lola said under her breath to Belle. Both were unabashedly staring at the love scene playing out across the room.

"You're jealous." It wasn't an accusation. But rather a statement. Lola had told her that she didn't want a relationship, but it was becoming obvious that she did.

"So what?" Lola shrugged. "My sister managed to snag one of the sexiest and most powerful men in the world, and he looks at her like he won the prize. Why wouldn't I be jealous?"

"You'll find him," Belle promised.

"I'm beginning to suspect that he doesn't exist." It was the first time she had admitted that part of her was still looking for Mr. Right.

"Trust me, you will. Probably when you least expect it."

"Speaking of…" Lola said dramatically. "I'll leave you two alone."

She hurried off as Smith made his way to his wife. Lola's sense of self-preservation was intact.

Belle couldn't help wondering if that was part of the problem as she watched Lola flee the scene. Then again, Belle herself had sworn off love, and she'd vowed never to go to bed with the cocky lawyer who hired her as a personal assistant.

Smith grinned at her as if he knew exactly where her thoughts were this Christmas morning. The two had a rocky start to their relationship, but that was the thing about love: it survived. Whatever metal love was made of was strong enough to thrive in even the most desolate circumstances. If they could find true love, then she had faith anyone could.

"Alexander beat me to the diamonds," Smith informed her. He wrapped an arm around Belle's waist and drew her to him.

"I don't need diamonds," she said. "I just need you."

That was the only price she had ever demanded of this man. His heart, his soul, his body, and he had given it all to her.

"Then I suppose I can take this back," he said. From behind her back, he drew a thin package.

"It isn't diamonds," he warned her as she opened it.

It was something far more perfect. The delicate charm bracelet, far more elegant than any she had seen before. There were only a few charms so far, but each of them meant something important to them. There was a tiny Empire State Building with incredible attention to details, a small feather and a star.

"I saw a couple more I'd like to add," he told her as he helped her put it on, "but I thought this was a good start."

"I love it."

"The two of you make a gorgeous couple," Aunt Jane interrupted unceremoniously, dropping her arms around each of them and pulling them into a group hug. "And that means you're going to make beautiful babies. So, when can I expect one?"

Aunt Jane was a force to be reckoned with in her own right. She had arrived in Scotland this morning with an overnight bag and a kaftan, only to promptly announce that she had a torrid affair to attend the next day. Belle wished she would stay longer, but she wasn't surprised. She was a woman of means. Although she had flitted from husband to husband and many affairs, she had no children of her own. Belle had become her surrogate daughter, so it only seemed natural for her to ask.

Smith opened his mouth, trying to figure out the gentlest way to tell her to back off. But before he could respond, Belle broke in, "We're working on it."

Jane's eyes glinted wickedly. There had never been any shame in her game. An announcement of a carnal nature might have made another person blush, but it only thrilled her. "I'd ask for details," she said, "but I'll settle for updates."

Alexander shook his head as he walked by. It was nothing new for Aunt Jane to get involved in other people's love lives. He owed her a debt of gratitude for being involved with his own. She had been a voice of reason when Clara needed guidance. For that, he would always be grateful, but he could do more than that. He could pass along the favor to the next couple in line.

Swooping upon Edward, he gripped his brother's arm, "Can I have a moment?"

With all of the guests, the brothers hadn't had a chance to speak since Alexander's arrival the day before. But Clara had made it pretty clear that Edward needed to speak to him.

Edward fidgeted a little before nodding to an empty alcove. It was rarely a good sign when a family member needed to speak to you in private on Christmas, but

Alexander's gut told him this wasn't going to be bad news.

"Clara talked to you?" Edward guessed as soon as they were alone.

Alexander nodded. The less he said the easier it would be for his brother to get this out.

"I don't know how much she told you," Edward began.

"Nothing," Alexander answered, "She insisted I speak directly to you." He didn't bother to hide the insinuation in his voice. His little brother wasn't going to get out of coming clean to him.

"David and I would like to get married," Edward said in a rush. This wasn't news to Alexander, but he waited patiently for his brother to continue. "On New Year's Eve, and we'd like you to marry us."

"If this King gig doesn't work out, I suppose I can become a minister," Alexander teased. This was the second wedding he'd been asked to officiate.

"Then you will?" Edward wiped a bead of sweat off his forehead, "And you'll give us permission?"

"I've had that document signed for ages, It's been so long that I can't even remember what I made David the duke of."

"You didn't have to do that," Edward said, his eyes shining.

"It's custom, and who am I to break with tradition?"

"Yes," Edward agreed, "that's my job."

"There's more," Alexander warned him. He didn't want to deliver troubling news to Edward on the cusp of his wedding, but he deserved to know. For the first time in a very long time, Alexander believed he could keep the information brief.

Edward listened quietly as Alexander filled him in on the details of the last few weeks.

"I know you have questions," Alexander said when he finished, "and I'll be happy to answer all of them. You deserve to know and so does he." He nodded to David.

"I haven't really kept him in the loop," Edward admitted.

That was Alexander's fault. He had been the one to dictate what could and could not be shared in his brother's relationship. That was a mistake. "I should never have asked you to keep anything from David."

Alexander had been learning this lesson recently himself, and he wouldn't stand by and force his brother to make the same mistake.

"I'm not sure how he will take it," Edward said. It was clear he was still digesting the news of Jacobson's capture and the existence of Anderson.

"Tell him anyway," Alexander advised. "It's for the best."

He clamped a hand on Edward's shoulder and then left him to consider this.

David found his fiancé still thinking in the corner a few minutes later. "Are you hiding or is something on your mind?"

"Lots of things," Edward said in a measured tone.

"I don't like how that sounds," David admitted.

"It won't change anything between the two of us," Edward prefaced. He needed David to know that. He had put the man he loved through hell, asked him to be patient with little guarantee of a happy ending, and broken his heart far too many times. "I just found out that my family is a little more fucked up than I thought."

David took his hands and squeezed them tightly. "I know the Royals are fucked up. If it bothered me, I would have been long gone a while ago." He tipped his head back toward the rest of the group, "Let's enjoy Christmas. Nothing you can tell me is going to change anything between the two of us, but I'm glad you want to share it with me."

Edward smiled, feeling a weight lift from his chest, "I want to share everything with you."

CHAPTER TWENTY-FOUR

ew Year's Eve arrived with a blanket of snow that covered the grounds of the castle. Thankfully, all the guests were in attendance for tonight's festivities, and Edward wouldn't have it any other way. While the extended family had returned to their homes in the city, those closest to him were scattered about Balmoral trying to keep warm. He'd already been down to the kitchen, only to be sent away by Mrs. Watson for attempting to snag a finger full of frosting. Apparently, even the groom-to-be wasn't allowed a taste test.

Much of the holiday decor transitioned nicely to a wedding. Although he'd added a few extra sprigs of holly in places. There wasn't much more he could do but count the hours.

Clara found him staring at a newspaper in the study a few hours later. She took a seat across from him, already dressed in a champagne-colored lace dress that accented the rich chestnut hues of her hair. Although her hair was done, her face was free of make-up. Despite that her pale skin glowed with unmistakable beauty.

"Afternoon shag?" he guessed, tossing aside the paper. He'd been rereading the same article without processing since he sat down. He had higher prospects of being entertained by his best friend.

"A nap," she said with a yawn, "and a shag." She stretched her slender arms over her head as though she was still waking up.

"I won't tell Alexander what order of preference you have for your daily activities," he said dryly. Not that it would matter in the least to his brother.

"What are you doing?" She eyed the abandoned newspaper as if he'd been up to no good.

"David has decided to be a traditionalist, and he refuses to see me before the wedding." Edward thought now was a peculiar time to adopt an ancient custom. They were blowing them all to hell just by getting married. If his entire married life was dependent on an archaic ritual, they were doomed.

Clara glanced around the room. "Where's Belle?"

"I loaned her to David," he explained. "I felt he needed a friend with him. It might be his idea not to see one another, but he's the possessive one in the relationship."

"Oh, really?" Clara couldn't hide her surprise, and Edward felt a slight surge of annoyance.

"In case it hasn't escaped your attention, I am not my brother."

220

"I noticed," she reassured him. "Well, if Belle has David duty, I get Edward duty."

"You sound like a nanny," he accused. There was nothing like feeling like a third wheel on his wedding day, but Clara shook her finger at him.

"I needed a nap, so I could stay up late," she said, "but now I'm all yours."

"I won't tell Alexander." Her explanation softened him. The truth was he was taking out his nerves on her. She didn't deserve that, especially if she wasn't feeling well. "Did Elizabeth keep you up?"

Clara shook her head, absentmindedly chewing on her lower lip. "She's finally sleeping through the night."

That meant Alexander had. Although he enjoyed teasing her about Alexander's libido, he didn't particularly want to know the details of his brother's intimate life.

"Let's get you dressed," Clara suggested, "and you could use a shave."

Edward felt along his jawline and grimaced. "This is why I need David around. I would have gone to the altar looking scruffy."

"In his future absence, you can use a mirror," she advised him as they set off for his bedroom.

Since David had insisted on tradition, Edward had taken his father's old bedroom. Plaid paper covered the walls in hues of navy and camel, and oak wainscoting lined the room's perimeter. Between the thick, canvas drapes and the hunting portraits, the entire space spoke to a repressed British masculinity that didn't suit him. Although Ralph Lauren might disagree.

"Is this what you're wearing?" Clara studied the tuxedo hanging on the wardrobe door.

"Yes." Edward swallowed a little as he looked at it. He supposed this what most women felt when they looked at their wedding gowns—a curious mixture of apprehension and excitement. It was classically cut with a double breast that reminded him of Cary Grant. He felt like he was stepping back in time whenever he wore it, but unlike the antiquated bedroom, it was into a period of glamour.

"You are going to look dashing."

It was exactly what he needed to hear.

"Are you nervous?" she asked, taking a chair by the door.

He shook his head, moving into the adjoin bath to start the hot tap on the sink. "Not exactly. I can't describe it really. I feel..."

"Ready?" she offered him.

That was exactly it. He was ready. It was strange that he had spent so much of his life denying who he was. It had been David that made him realize he didn't want to be anyone else save a man who could deserve David's love. "Yes, but I'm still anxious. I know that doesn't make sense. I keep thinking David will come to his senses and bolt."

"David has been ready to drag you to the altar for years," Clara reminded him. "He's not going to bolt now."

Still. Edward went to the bar cart his father had always kept well-stocked and poured two glasses of Scotch. A drink couldn't hurt to steady his nerves. It was a tradition he didn't mind observing, but when he held one out to Clara, she shook her head.

"None for me. It will put me to sleep. Alexander kept me up all night." She yawned for good measure, but Edward saw through it.

"Not drinking and afternoon naps?" he pointed out.

She did her best to feign innocence. "It is the holiday season."

"Don't make me read about it on the tabloids." The royal bump watch was due to start up any day now that Elizabeth was walking. Apparently, Clara had seen fit to give them something to actually watch.

"We haven't told anyone," she said in a low voice. "I thought we would wait a little longer."

His eyebrows knit in confusion, and he brushed a rogue curl from his forehead. Then it dawned on him. She didn't want to upset Belle. The third member of the trio wanted a baby as well. While it wouldn't surprise anyone that knew Clara was pregnant once more, he understood her desire to keep it to herself.

"Your secret is safe with me," he promised.

"What secret?" Alexander demanded, poking his head into the room.

"It wouldn't be a secret if I told you," Edward explained.

"I'll leave you two for a bit." Clara excused herself, and Alexander's eyes followed her out of the room.

"She's only in the hallway," Edward reassured him. Sometimes he thought his brother might fade into nothing without the presence of his wife, and yet, their love was a comforting reminder that the real thing still existed.

"I came to give you a pep talk since Dad isn't here," Alexander said. "But then I remembered how uplifting his pep talk was when I got married."

"I thought he threatened you." Edward recollected that he'd been asked to leave the room that morning. It was the last time he had spoken to his father until the church. A shiver ran down his spine at the memory. Today would be different. That's precisely why Edward had wanted it this way.

"He did, mostly." Alexander smiled sadly. "But he also told me about marriage. I didn't pay much attention to him, to be honest. I wish I had now." He paused for a long moment as if paying a silent tribute to him. "What I do know is that you and David will be fine."

"Is that it?" Edward couldn't help but laugh.

"I thought about giving you advice about your wedding night duties, but I didn't think I was the expert there." Alexander gave him a meaningful look, and they both laughed. "If you are willing to fight for each other, you'll make it through. All you need is love and a lot of stubbornness."

The Cambridge men had that in spades.

Alexander pulled an envelope out of his pocket. "Your official documentation. I've signed and stamped and decreed."

Edward pulled the papers out and stared at them. This was actually happening.

"I couldn't decide if I could make you both the Duke of York," Alexander explained, "so I thought I'd ask you."

Edward grinned at the thought of the two Dukes of York. It was certainly a new precedent that he was about to set. "I'll ask David."

There was no pressing need to decide right now. For a few blissful days they would be able to keep their marriage private. Eventually, the world would weigh in but tonight was about love. Everything else could wait. He'd struggled a lifetime to get to this place, and soon, with his friends and family, at his side, he would finally be home.

CHAPTER TWENTY-FIVE

*B*elle didn't like being apart from Smith, especially on their anniversary, but today it couldn't be avoided. Edward had insisted she keep an eye on David, but she had other concerns preoccupying her. That's how the two had wound up in the village only a few hours prior to the wedding.

"I'm glad you don't need your hair or make-up done," she confessed to David as they parked their borrowed Range Rover in front of a row of shops.

"It's my complexion," he teased.

She couldn't disagree. The rich hue of his skin accented his cheekbones and jawline. "It's actually a shame that you and Edward can't have babies biologically. They would be gorgeous."

"Don't I know it?" David said with a blinding grin. He was in a friendly mood today. Although the two had spent time together before, they never had a chance to bond outside the presence of their other friends. When she'd called upon him for help, he had jumped at the chance. Maybe he was as eager to get to know her as she was to get to know him. Of course, it could also have something to do with their secret mission.

"Speaking of…" Belle squared her shoulders and turned to study the shop windows.

"It's over there." David pointed to a small store at the corner. Grabbing her hand, he dragged her toward it.

It was hard to say which of the two of them was more excited.

"You know," Belle said breathlessly as they stepped into the pharmacy, "by next week, you'll be all over the tabloids if you get caught dragging a blonde into a pharmacy."

"Imagine if they caught a snap of this!" He tossed her a long, blue box from the shelf. If the thought of being hounded by the paparazzi bothered him, he didn't show it. Edward had done a fair job keeping the press away from him, but once they were married all bets were off. "Should you do it here or back there?"

"I think I better pay for it," she said with a laugh.

The cashier rang them up, glancing in confusion at the two of them. Belle realized she was wearing a wedding band and David wasn't. Rather than explain herself, she simply crossed her fingers for dramatic effect and dashed out of the shop with the bag.

David followed her, almost doubled over. "She's still scratching her head."

"I don't see why it was so strange." Belle felt inexplicably indignant over the whole thing.

"I've been holding hands with Edward in there all month," he reminded her.

"Well, then, we're just one big, happy family, aren't we?" Belle planted her hands on her hips and tossed her hair.

"I couldn't agree more."

SHE STARED AT THE STRIP, sitting in the locked bathroom. Despite his enthusiasm, David had understood why she wanted to tell her husband first. How long could these bloody things take anyway? But within a matter of moments, a second line began to appear. It was faint. Belle turned the test around, trying to make certain it wasn't a trick of the light.

Two lines.

She could see it. She could say it. But she couldn't seem to believe it. There was only one way to make this feel real to her. She needed Smith.

It took her longer than she would have liked to track down a pair of boots and some gloves. When Smith had decided to go out with the gameskeeper, she had thought it would be the perfect opportunity to sneak into the village without him. She couldn't bear disappointing him if the test had come back negative, but it wasn't negative. It was positive.

"I'm pregnant," she said to the empty room as she

tugged on the boots. The room didn't respond. The room was not being helpful.

She had less than two hours until the wedding, and maybe it was stark raving mad, but she was going out into the Scottish tundra to track down her husband. She simply couldn't wait any longer. Damn reason and common sense.

Norris gawked at her when she reached the door wearing the galoshes and one of Smith's overcoats. Her own outerwear was more pretty than practical. That would have to change, she realized. Now, she was dressing for two. She couldn't be without hats and socks and other important protection from the elements. Somewhere inside her a tiny voice reminded her that the baby was probably the size of the speck of dust, but it didn't matter. If she read that wearing bubble wrap was good for the baby, she would. It was a very good thing she'd insisted on staying behind the scenes at Bless. She could only imagine what her clients would think of that.

"Mrs. Price, can I drive you somewhere?" Norris offered.

She shook her head. "I need to find Smith."

"I'm sure he will return shortly." Norris tried to steer her from the door. "I don't think he would want you out in the cold."

It hardly mattered what either man wanted. She was going to do this. "Thank you, but I'll be fine."

Either she scared him or he decided it wasn't worth it to upset a woman on a wedding day—even if it wasn't her wedding day—because he backed down.

Outside it was significantly colder than Belle had realized. She prided herself on being an indoor girl. Although
she'd spent parts of her youth in the country, she usually
stayed out of the cold. Belle could cope with a dusting of
snow, this was much more. Her feet sank as she stepped
onto the grounds, the snow coming past her ankles.
Finding the boots had been a very good idea even if they
didn't do much against the cold. She was fairly certain she
had frostbite before she even got a hundred meters further.

She had just resolved to turn back when a Range Rover
rumbled toward the house. It broke as soon as it saw her, and
the door swung open. Smith jumped out and rushed to her.

"What on earth are you doing out here?" The more time
he spent with the staff, the thicker the traces of his Scottish
accent became.

Maybe this was where they should get a proper house
for the baby, Belle thought. Smith seemed at home here.
She had never imagined that she would want an estate of
her own. Now it seemed necessary. Then again, there was
the issue of snow.

"Belle!" Smith grabbed her by the shoulders. "Your lips
are blue. Let's get you inside."

It wasn't until he said it that she realized just how
frozen her lips had become. She wasn't even certain she
could speak. Although she hadn't made it very far from the
house, he insisted she ride back in the Rover. As soon as
they were through the front door, he swept her off her feet
and carried her to their bedroom.

Smith knelt before her and took off her boots, rubbing her toes until blood started to flow again.

"What were you thinking?" he asked, not able to keep a bemused grin from his face.

Belle looked into his green eyes, losing herself for only a moment. Would the baby have those eyes? The thought stirred her back to life and the rest of the chill began to melt away. The trouble was that Smith wouldn't stay still long enough to tell him.

First, he insisted on starting a fire. Then he found her socks. He called to the kitchen for hot tea.

"I am not an invalid," she called after him when he inquired with the butler about a hot water bottle.

"What were you doing out there?" he asked, carrying the cup and saucer to the bedside table.

"I needed to find you," she began.

"I was coming back, beautiful." He tucked a few, loose strands of hair behind her ears.

"We should be together for our anniversary." Why couldn't she just bring herself to say it? Perhaps because the more she saw her outing through Smith's eyes, the more she understood it. Would her whole pregnancy be filled with random acts of insanity?

The butler reappeared with the water bottle and Smith excused himself to the loo to fill it. He was through the door before it registered with Belle. She sat up in the bed. This was the second time in a month that she'd left something lying around that she shouldn't. This time the look on Smith's face when he wandered back into the room was very different than the first.

He was still staring at the test, a curious mixture of wonder and shock plastered on his face.

"Beautiful?" He looked up to her, his eyes full of questions.

She bit her lip and nodded. "I came out to tell you, but I think the words got frozen along with my toes. Happy Anniversary."

"Are your toes okay?" He dropped the test on the bed and reached for her feet. "Do you need me to rub them? Are you hungry? Maybe you should lie down?"

"I don't think we can do the whole nine months in one day," she said with a laugh. Her hands reached out to beckon him to her. Smith climbed into the bed beside her and wrapped his arms around her. They stayed like that for a few minutes until Smith laid down, placing his head in her lap. Turning to her belly, he places a soft kiss where his child grew. Then he slowly began to sing. Tears prickled Belle's eyes as she recognized it. It was as bittersweet as their story, but as filled with promises, too. When he finished, they stayed like that, dreaming of the future.

CHAPTER TWENTY-SIX

*W*ith no bride present, the grooms decided to eschew tradition and escort themselves to the altar. Clara led the party with Elizabeth in her arms. Unfortunately, the flower girl was more interested in eating the rose petals than dropping them. I couldn't help but stare at my wife as she made her way across the room. There was none of the pomp and circumstance of our wedding, and somehow the intimacy of the event seemed to erase that fateful day.

When Edward had first shared his plans to marry David, my only concern had been regarding his security. Now I knew that my family was safe, which left me free to focus on the happiness that I'd been robbed of on my own wedding day.

Edward and David entered through doors on the opposite side of the room and walked slowly toward one another, stopping when they reached me. We'd chosen the parlor because the Christmas tree provided a beautiful backdrop. Someone had snuck in earlier in the day and removed most of the ornaments in favor of dozens of white roses tucked into the evergreen branches.

"Please join hands," I instructed the two, shooting Edward a wink. He wanted a traditional wedding, and I would do my best to give it to him. "I was told to keep this short, because Mrs. Watson made a cake."

Edward rolled his eyes, but everyone else laughed. If my little brother thought he was going to get away without being embarrassed, he was mistaken. I considered it part of my official role. My brother looked dashing in his classic tuxedo while David had opted for a more modern cut. Somehow the contrast seemed to fit them as perfectly as they fit one another.

"Over the last few days I've shared some thoughts about marriage with Edward, and he told me I wasn't very helpful. I think Clara might agree with that assessment." She nodded vigorously but she couldn't keep a smile off her face. "So, I decided I wouldn't talk about marriage, I would talk about love. But only for a few minutes, so we can all have cake."

"Thank God," Edward interjected.

"I used to believe that love was a fairytale," I began, "and maybe I was right, because one day, a princess walked into my life. She made me believe in love. She brought so many of us together. Edward once thanked me for showing the courage to choose love over duty or tradition. But she was the one who was strong enough to break away from the expectations and the fear. Before I met her, I felt alone. Now she will always be with me. That's what love is: a constant companion, a best friend who sticks beside you, a soft place to call home. She showed me that. That's why love is so powerful: it can never be broken, even when one of you breaks. Love never loses faith, even when there is nothing left to believe in. Love shines a light, even in the darkest hours. All of us are searching for our happily ever after, but the luckiest of us know that it isn't a place or a destiny. Happily ever after is a person. I know my brother has found his, which is why I couldn't be more proud to stand by him today."

Edward dropped David's hands and hugged me. Pulling back, there were tears in his eyes. "Thank you."

When he had stepped back into place, I couldn't help myself. "I think I'm supposed to ask if anyone objects."

"On with it!" Edward demanded with a laugh.

I led them through their vows, and when the time came, I happily looked to my brother and told him, "You may kiss your husband."

Cheers erupted from everyone, and when Edward and David finally released one another, love shining in their eyes, the crowd gathered for a hug. Clara broke away from the group and came to my side.

"How did I do?" I asked, sweeping her into my arms.

"You made me want to marry you all over again." She pressed up onto her toes and gave me a quick kiss.

"I could do without another wedding," I told her. "Would you settle for a lifetime, poppet?"

"How about a happily ever after?" she whispered.

"Do you think they'll miss us?"

Clara glanced at our loved ones and shook her head. I swept her into my arms and carried her from the room. Pausing at the base of the stairs, I brought my mouth to hers. It was the kiss we should have shared on our own wedding day. Our lips sealed to one another, her breath becoming my own and my life becoming hers.

When we broke apart, I took the stairs slowly, unable to look away from her. In her eyes, I found all the answers I had ever sought. I had been broken until the day she stumbled into my life, and her love fused my shattered pieces. She gave me faith when I deserved none. In all the darkness of my past I found an angel, and she guided me home. When I least expected it, she completed me.

ACKNOWLEDGMENTS

Writing the Royals for the last three years has been an amazing experience. I could never have predicted how these books would change my life, and I've been so blessed to go on this journey with friends and family. Some were here at the beginning and others I picked up along the way. I couldn't have down it without any of them.

A big thank you to Louise Fury, who lives up to her name! I'm not certain why my delirious, jet-lag induced ramblings impressed you, but I'm so glad you took a chance on me. I have a feeling that this is the beginning of a beautiful friendship.

Darling Elise, I could not live without you. Literally. I might die as you often feed me when I'm writing. Thank you for everything you do—and you do everything! You are the best business partner, therapist, little sister I could ask for.

Thanks to Stephanie for staying on top of all the day-to-day realities when I'm in another world. I couldn't do this without you.

I have some of the best foreign publishers in the world. To the team at Blanvalet Verlag, you have made my wildest dreams come true. Thank you to Wiebke for championing my books. I owe you so much. And thanks to Berit for being an all-around awesome publicist and friend. I'll never forget the time we spent traveling, and I can't wait for you to come visit us in Washington!

Thank you to Hugo & Cie for the beautiful French editions of the Royals. Big hugs to Hughe for bringing romance novels to France. Your ideas are as big as your heart!

I'm so blessed to count myself amongst the Inkslinger family. Thank you to KP for being a true friend and trusted source of wisdom, and thanks to Jessica for putting up with me, which is no easy feat.

I've made so many friends along this journey that I could fill another book with their names. But I need to say thank you to a few. To Shayla, you are the best. Thank you for always reminding me to take no shit. To Rebecca, you are a very big fish. Thank you for keeping me grounded. To Irina, thank you for your time and your talents.

I owe so much to my Loves. From those of you who were part of GLRC to now, I can always count on you to make me smile and keep me motivated. Thank you!

Thank you to all the bloggers, who give their time self-lessly to support books. I couldn't do this without you.

I have the most supportive family in the world. They

are my rock when I need something to cling to, and my driving force when I need a gentle shove. My children are the reason for everything I do. I love you. To Josh, thank you for sharing me with Alexander and Smith for the last three years. All of my heart belongs to you. I could not do any of this without you by my side.

And to my readers, thank you—for being part of this story. The Royals belong to all of you, because you loved them and believed them. You made them real, and I can never show you enough appreciation for that gift. Thank you for reading. This book is paper and ink, and you are its soul.

ABOUT THE AUTHOR

Geneva Lee is the *New York Times, USA Today,* and internationally bestselling author of over a dozen novels. Her bestselling Royals Saga has sold over one million copies worldwide. She is the co-owner of Away With Words, a destination bookstore in Poulsbo, Washington. When she isn't traveling, she can usually be found writing, reading, or buying another pair of shoes.

Learn more about Geneva Lee at:
www.GenevaLee.com